A Gangsta's Love Language

A Patton Brothers Spin-Off

K.L. Hall

B. Love Publications

BLP

Visit bit.ly/readBLP to join our mailing list for sneak peeks and release day links!

Let's connect on social media!
Facebook - B. Love Publications
Twitter - @blovepub
Instagram - @blovepublications

We hate errors, but we are human! If the B. Love team leaves any grammatical errors behind, do us a kindness and send them to us directly in an email to blovepublications@gmail.com **with ERRORS as the subject line.**

As always, if you enjoyed this book, please leave a review on Amazon/Goodreads, recommend it on social media and/or to a friend, and mark it as READ on your Goodreads profile.

A Gangsta's Love Language
Synopsis

When it came time for Kendrick "XL" Patton to pick between life and death, he chose me.

But with a life-threatening health diagnosis looming over me, I was already prepared to meet my maker.

Until he offered to marry me to save my life.

Talk about a plot twist.

Initially, I thought the idea was foolish.

Who the hell marries a stranger to get health insurance?

I do, apparently, and in more ways than one.

It's only a marriage on paper. It doesn't mean anything.

But as we settle into our secret arrangement, our chemistry becomes impossible to ignore, like a slow-smoldering fire that only strengthens.

Living in such close proximity makes it hard to turn a blind eye to how good his soft lips feel against mine or how his rugged hands grip me like he'll never let go.

Before long, our hearts refuse to be ignored, taking control and leading us into uncharted waters.

Who knows, maybe becoming Mrs. Patton might be the best mistake I ever made.

A Gangsta's Love Language is a standalone novel and part of the Patton Brothers series.

Prologue

K endrick "XL" Patton

AMIR, AHSAN, AND I STOOD IN SILENCE, WATCHING RICO TAKE his last breath. The minute his body stopped twitching, I stepped forward, my expression critical. "There's something else y'all need to know," I murmured.

My cousins shifted their necks toward each other before looking at me with frowns creasing their foreheads. "What is it?" Amir asked first.

Instead of responding, I gestured toward the warehouse door. "Come outside with me."

The three of us trekked outside into the night. I felt the bite of the secret I held gnawing at my gut. I led them to my car and popped the trunk. Inside, a woman was knocked out and bound by the wrists and ankles.

Amir shifted his weight from one foot to the other. "Who the fuck is she?"

"She was with Rico," I explained. "She saw me when I went to get him, so I had to take her too."

Ahsan looked at the woman, then back at me. "Is she dead?"

I swung my head in a no. "No, she's very much alive. For now."

Amir paused, trying to quickly process the new situation I'd presented. "Then you already know what you need to do," he said, his voice hard as stone.

I dipped my chin, understanding the gravity of the situation. "Yeah, I do."

"Good. Then it's settled."

I closed the trunk and maneuvered around the car to the driver's seat. The night was dark, and the ride was silent. The only sound was the engine's growl as I sped down the road, headed for the desert. I gripped the steering wheel tightly, focusing only on the task at hand. The unconscious woman in my trunk was a key witness who'd seen too much, and she had to be handled. It wasn't as if I'd never taken a life before. It was just another part of the game and the role I'd been chosen to play.

I drove to an undisclosed location—a remote spot deep in the Mojave Desert, far from probing eyes. I parked the car, grabbed my gun from underneath the seat, and continued on to the trunk. I opened the lid with a deep breath, revealing the woman whose body began to stir. Her eyelids slowly fluttered open. I expected to see fear, but instead, she looked up at me with a lack of protest as if she already knew how the rest of the night would unfold. I quickly raised my gun, ready to pull the trigger and put a quick end to things. But before I could, she spoke, her voice weak but direct.

"You should know I'm already dying."

I hesitated, her words catching me off guard. "What the fuck did you just say?" I asked with a grunt.

"I'm dying. So, even if you don't kill me, my rare blood disorder surely will."

I lowered the gun slightly as doubt and curiosity mixed with my usual emotional detachment. I knew a mothafucka would say anything to dodge a bullet with their name on it, but I still couldn't help but probe. "What kind of disorder?"

She looked up at me, her fiery gaze filled with defiance. "It's a lot of big, scary, long words that mean blood clots are forming in small blood vessels throughout my body. Without treatment, I'm knocking on death's door."

"Death comes for us all. When it's your time, all a real nigga can do is be ready."

"When you're right, you're right. All I wanted to do was get even with Rico before I died."

My grip on the gun loosened as I processed her words. I'd been in the game long enough to see through lies and recognize the truth. "You were trying to get even with Rico? For what?"

She nodded again, her expression hardening. "Yeah, but I guess it doesn't matter now. Do your worst."

I gave her a onceover with the gun still in my hand. Something in her words and the raw honesty of her situation made me hold back. Instead of pulling the trigger, I lowered the gun entirely and reversed my steps. I looked at her body, still curled into the fetal position, and my curiosity awakened. I needed to know what made her so willing to face me and death with such courage.

"What issue did you have with Rico?" I inquired.

She took a deep breath, her eyes filled with pain. "I hate that mothafucka with every breath I have in me. He betrayed my twin brother. He set him up and made him look like a traitor. My brother ended up in the hospital with ten bullets in him. On his third day in ICU, he died. He always said he never thought he'd see thirty, but I didn't want to believe it was true."

My expression shifted slightly, a hint of empathy in my otherwise hardened features. I knew about the ruthlessness in Rico's blood, but hearing it from a stranger's perspective brought a new layer of understanding.

I slightly bowed my chin. "I'm sorry to hear that. How old was he when he passed?"

She continued, her voice steady despite the bare emotion in her words. "Almost twenty-four. A month later, I got sick, and these flat, red spots started popping up all over my body. I thought it was a bad flare-up from my Lupus, but when I couldn't shake my fever for four days, I broke down and went to the emergency room. They ran some tests and told me I have some crazy, rare blood disorder called thrombotic thrombocytopenic purpura. Talk about a mouthful. I don't have the right type of enzyme in my blood, and I likely got it because of my Lupus," she explained.

I agreed. "That is a mouthful."

"They wanted to start me on medication and these expensive ass plasma treatments, but without health insurance, and the treatments being over a thousand dollars per procedure, I said no thanks. I'll take my chances with death. In doing so, I said fuck it and vowed to get vengeance for Zo before I died. I couldn't let Rico's bitch ass get away with it."

I processed her story, feeling a strange blend of respect and empathy for her. Even though I didn't know her, I shared the same unwavering determination to right the wrongs done to my family. It was why I'd personally hand delivered Rico to Ahsan for what he did to him.

"You don't have to worry about Rico anymore. He's been taken care of. You ain't the only one out here who wanted that bitch nigga to meet his maker," I stated with a grunt.

She nodded, a grim smile forming on her lips. "Good. What was your beef with Rico? Must've been something just as bad if it made you wanna come all the way to Miami to kill him."

"He shot and robbed my cousin," I answered.

"Did he die too?"

I swung my head in a no. "Nah. He pulled through."

"Good." She paused before grunting as if the darkest thoughts were playing in her head. "I hope he fucking burns in Hell. Rico, that is. Not your cousin."

I tucked my gun away completely, no longer seeing her as a loose end but as an ally against a common enemy. At that moment, I made an impulsive decision. I couldn't change the past, but I could choose a different path for the future of the woman before me.

I extended my hand to help her out of the trunk. "It's okay. I don't plan on killing you tonight."

"But it's not completely off the table, right?" she asked as she reluctantly grabbed my hand.

Once out, she dusted off her clothes and looked up at me. My heart somersaulted in my chest. She was fucking gorgeous. She stood at about five-foot-five with butterscotch brown skin. Her hair was swept up into two space buns with sleek baby hairs and curly ringlets framing her round face. Her brows were thick and well-manicured, and long, wispy lashes sat overtop her deep-set brown eyes. A constellation of light brown freckles graced the bridge of her button nose, and a small stud set nestled in her left nostril. A small medusa piercing sparkled just above the cupid's bow on her full lips.

"You told me to do my worst, but I won't. Tell me more about your illness. Maybe there's something I can do to help."

She looked at me with surprise before shrugging her shoulders. "Help? Do you not know what the words life-threatening mean?"

"Humor me."

She turned away, and I noticed the rose tattoo on her neck.

"What more is there to tell? I already said that I won't be around much longer without those plasma exchanges. The bullshit waitressing job I have in Miami doesn't offer health insurance, and I don't have enough money to pay for my rent *and* my medication and treatment. So, right now, living feels impossible. I'm ready to give the fuck up. To not stress or worry anymore. To not have so much hate inside me, eating away at my heart from the inside out," she confessed, venting her emotions and frustrations to me as if I was her therapist.

The vulnerability in her voice made my hitman facade slowly melt away. I didn't believe in much, but our meeting started to feel like divine intervention, fate, or something out of this world. I could almost feel Big Mama's presence looming over me, coaxing me to do the right thing.

"So, you're saying there's a chance to save you, but you just need money for the treatments?"

She nodded, her eyes brimming with a twinge of hope. "It's a long shot at this point, but maybe so if I can get the medication and plasma treatments. If those don't work, the last option is spleen surgery."

My expression changed. I'd seen the harsh realities of life, but hearing her struggle touched a part of me I thought I'd long buried. I stood in silence for a moment, my mind racing. Then, an idea struck me out of the blue—something that could change everything for both of us.

"What if I offered you access to my health insurance?"

She snapped her neck at me, expression filled with confusion. "Your health insurance? How would that even work?"

My chest inflated with a deep breath, knowing how crazy the words would sound coming out of my mouth and recognizing the life-changing opportunity they'd present. "Marry me. If we get married, you'll have access to my health insurance, which can cover your treatments."

She froze, features chilled with shock, staring at me with her eyes popped wide. The idea was crazy and unexpected, yet I saw a flicker of hope light up her eyes. Deep down, we both knew she didn't want to die. *Maybe, just maybe, this could work.*

"Marry you? You were just seconds away from killing me, and now you're asking me to... this is... this is insane."

I shrugged, a small, almost apologetic smile on my full lips. "Yeah, it is. But sometimes, the craziest ideas are the ones that generate the best outcomes."

She paused, thinking about it as if she had any other options. I knew the logical part of her mind was screaming against my impromptu proposal. Mine was too. But in my heart, I knew it might've been her last shot. She looked up at me, seeing the sincerity in my eyes.

"You don't even know my name. You don't know shit about me."

"Then tell me."

"Zahra."

"I'm Kendrick, but everybody calls me XL."

"Why XL?"

I looked down at myself, wondering if she could see me. "I'd always been a big nigga with more fat than muscle as a child. I didn't start lifting weights until high school but never lost my burliness."

"Got it," she replied, looking around at the mountains and desert surrounding us. "Where are we?"

"Vegas."

She shuffled back a step or two, almost losing her balance. "Are you serious?"

"As a heart attack."

"Holy shit. I'm a long way from home."

"Yeah. I know."

"And if I said yes... to marrying you, would this be strictly on paper? Just like... a marriage of convenience? Because I'm not looking for a Prince Charming to swoop in and save me."

"Good, because this ain't a fairytale."

She pressed her full lips together before licking them. "Okay. I'll do it. I'll marry you."

I nodded, understanding the gravity of our agreement. Our unlikely alliance, born out of desperation and hatred for Rico, might've just been the key to saving Zahra's life and giving us both a chance at redemption.

XI

T*hree months later.*

I'D BEEN SECRETLY HIDING ZAHRA IN MY APARTMENT SINCE I brought her back from Miami and married her. My daily routine had become a tailored dance between my responsibilities with my businesses, family, and secret marital arrangement. My double life required constant attention, and I was still learning to navigate the twists and turns of my new reality.

Every morning, I arrived at my restaurant before the doors opened, ensuring everything was in order and to my liking. Violet's was a cozy yet upscale soul food establishment on Ahsan's land. I was busting my ass to be sure all of Big Mama's mouth-watering recipes were known all around the city and beyond. I had the respect of my staff, not just as a boss but as a leader, making a name for myself in the culinary industry, one dish at a time.

I reviewed the daily specials with my sous chef, checking the inventory and ensuring the spotless dining area. My sharp eye for detail and hands-on approach kept everything running to my liking.

My afternoons were spent at the barbershop, a known staple in the city where regulars and celebrities alike came to get fresh. My barbershop was my first business—my baby.

Becoming a business owner in my twenties made me a man. It was the first thing I became responsible for, which was a big difference from my responsibilities in the game. My hand moved precisely, delivering detailed, error-free cuts while engaging in typical barbershop banter with my clients. I enjoyed the moments of normalcy, where the hum of my clippers offered a brief escape from the weight of my secret home life. Yet, behind my composed exterior, my thoughts often drifted to Zahra and her health.

Behind closed doors, my nights were a different story. After the barbershop doors closed, I visited the hospital to see Zahra. She'd been staying there while she received her plasma treatments. Our "marriage," born out of necessity, had no emotional ties or rings. Yet, we'd formed a friendship, and had grown accustomed to doing things together, like talking about our days while she ate the food I brought her from the restaurant and binge-watched some wild new reality show she was into. I was there so often that the nurses on her floor knew me on a first name basis. Since they'd done such a good job ensuring Zahra always had everything she needed, I showed my appreciation by giving each of them a twenty percent discount to use whenever they came to eat at my restaurant.

Most nights, when I got home alone, I reflected on how drastically my life had changed within a few months. I was the nigga who used to live solely for my own survival and profit. Now, I was secretly married to a woman I still didn't know but was entangled in the fight to save her life. It was a gamble, but for the first time, I felt motivated to do something for someone past my benefit—something I hadn't felt since before I lost Big Mama.

I arrived at the twenty-four-seven pool hall, a familiar spot where I often met up with my cousins. As usual, the place was buzzing with the nighttime rush, but I quickly spotted Ahsan and Amir stationed at a corner table with their pool cues in hand, deep in conversation.

Ahsan smiled with satisfaction as I approached. "It's about time you got here."

"Wassup, yo?" I greeted them both.

Amir reached out to dap me up. "Wassup, XL?"

Ahsan followed suit. "Ain't shit, just getting ready to bust y'all asses in a game of pool."

"I got first," I announced while grabbing a pool stick off the rack. "How's lil man?" I asked Amir.

Amir looked down at his phone, a broad grin spreading across his bearded face as he flipped it around to me. On his screensaver was a candid picture of Nerissa and the baby sleeping. "He's perfect."

I leaned in, my tough exterior softening as I looked at the tiny bundle of joy nestled in Nerissa's arms. "That's wassup. I've been meaning to get over to the house to see him, but between the restaurant and the barbershop, you know how shit goes."

Amir nodded. "I understand. We all got a lot of shit going on."

"How's fatherhood treating you, though? Any complaints?"

Amir chuckled. "It's exhausting as hell but worth it. Plus you know we're also planning the wedding. It's been crazy, but we're making it happen."

I patted him on the back. "That's wassup. And what about you, father-to-be?" I asked, turning my attention to Ahsan. "How's Sienna doing?"

"You know her, keeping me on my toes as always. But she's in the second trimester now. It's both exciting and nerve-racking."

"I can only imagine."

I chuckled outwardly, while on the inside, feeling a pang of longing for the simpler, happier aspects of life that my cousins were experiencing. Still, I wasn't a hater.

"So, when are you gon' settle down?" Ahsan probed. "You're the only one left, man."

I leaned forward to take my shot while masking my initial surprise. Those niggas hardly ever probed into my love life. But somehow, his question hit closer to home more than ever.

I played it off with a smirk before sinking my striped ball into the corner pocket. "You know I've always been a bit of a lone wolf," I replied with a lazy shrug.

Amir arched a questioning brow. "C'mon, yo. There's gotta be somebody on your line. You can't keep dodging commitment forever."

My thoughts drifted to Zahra and our unconventional but maturing bond. No matter how badly I wanted to, I couldn't share everything with my cousins.

"Don't worry about me. I'm good," I assured them before taking my next shot.

On one level, I felt a nagging guilt about keeping Zahra a secret. My cousins were like brothers to me, and their openness about their lives only highlighted my secrecy. I hated lying, especially to my family, but my situation was far from normal. Zahra had blown into my life under extreme circumstances, and the details of our relationship were too tricky to put into words, especially when they both knew I was supposed to have killed her. The guilt lingered, a continuous reminder of the double life I was juggling.

I'd become an expert at justifying my actions, though. I'd assured myself I was doing the right thing by keeping her hidden. I'd convinced myself that I wasn't technically lying to anyone as long as I didn't mention Zahra. That way, I was protecting her as well as my family. The justification was how I slept at night, believing that my silence was a form of safeguarding everyone I cared about.

While lost in my thoughts, Amir's phone buzzed with a new message. He glanced down, his brows furrowing as he read the text.

His eyes traveled left to right before jerking his head toward us. "Fuck."

"What is it?" I asked. "Everything good with Nerissa and the baby?"

"Yeah, it's not them. It's fuckin' Brandi, yo," he grumbled.

"Brandi? I thought I'd never have to hear that fuckin' name again," Ahsan grumbled.

I snapped out of my trance, my attention fully captured as I nodded in agreement. "Right."

"Somebody just sent me this," he said, turning the phone's screen toward me.

The three of us huddled to watch a reel she'd posted to her Instagram account of her relaxing on a tropical beach in the arms of a nigga none of us had seen in at least ten, maybe fifteen years—Cannon Walker.

He was an ex-dealer turned government informant. He was charged with possession with intent to distribute. The Feds executed a search warrant at his crib and recovered the works—cocaine, over $20,000 in cash, and jewelry. He flipped on his entire operation in exchange for his freedom, taking a plea deal. Last we'd heard, he fled Nevada and went south toward Florida.

Brandi's caption read: *My baby, my slime, my everything. This is a different type of love. Better than the last. Thank God I came to my senses and am happier than ever.*

"What the fuck? She's with that nigga now?"

Amir sucked his teeth. "I already know this is payback for me moving on with Rizzy."

"I thought you handled her ass when you broke things off," Ahsan stated.

"Thought I did too. Vegas bitches are crazy as hell these days."

My eyes narrowed, my protective instincts surging to the forefront. Brandi's unpredictably, petty ass was a complication none of us needed. "We need to watch her. She's playing with fire, and she thinks this shit is cute."

"She knows shit that could blow back on all of us if she runs her mouth to him," Amir added.

Ahsan and I nodded in agreement, the weight of the situation crystal clear. "Agreed. We can't let this get out of hand. Let's keep a close eye on her moves for now," Ahsan stated before looking down at his phone. "It's Sienna. I'll be right back."

I nodded before turning my attention back to Amir. "I'll ask around, see if anyone's got more details," I offered. "We can't afford any loose ends."

"You're right about that. Shit has been smooth as butter in our lives for a few months now. I'm trying to keep it that way."

"Me too." Ahsan returned to the table minutes later with a scowl on his expression. "What's wrong?" I asked, stopping our game to look at him with concern.

"Sienna just told me the gallery with her artwork on display here in Vegas was broken into and vandalized. She said somebody spray painted the words *You can't have it all* on the wall where her paintings were on display ruining them, and even stealing some."

My heart sank. "Oh shit."

Amir's brows snapped together. "Who the fuck would do some shit like that?"

"I don't know, but I'm pissed as hell. I told her I was on my way home. I don't want her stressing out over this shit, especially when she's carrying my baby."

Amir and I nodded without hesitation. "Go be with your wife, nigga," his brother advised.

"Exactly," I added. "We're good here. Keep us posted."

"I will."

Ahsan grabbed his jacket and raced out of the pool hall. Amir turned to look at me. "Guess I spoke too soon about shit being good."

"I guess you did, nigga."

Zahra Adams-Patton

What would you do if you found out you had a rare disorder and only had a small window of time left to live? Would you make amends with everyone you ever wronged to be the best version of yourself in your final days, or would you serve up a big, sloppy middle finger to everyone who ever wronged you or the ones you loved and make them pay? I chose the latter to avenge the only man who had a piece of my heart—my twin brother, Lorenzo.

I took my first breath at four o'clock on a rainy spring morning. Two minutes later, Zo took his. We were more than siblings who shared the same birthday. We were best friends. He was the peanut butter to my jelly and the Robin to my Batman. Nobody understood the bond between people like us unless they were born twins. The connection my brother and I shared was everything.

We were born and raised in Miami. From the culture to the warm weather, he and I were Florida babies to our core. From birth, we did everything together, supporting each other through the highs and lows of adolescence—from our first diaper rashes to our first prom dates. Lorenzo was the one person I could always count on, and our connection was unbreakable.

It was no surprise his death hit me like a freight train. I had Rico to thank for that. I hated him ever since my brother first brought him to my attention. He was some snake from Vegas who'd come to Miami looking for a quick come-up. He was introduced to my brother through a mutual friend, and lucky for Rico, they hit it off. Lorenzo was gullible like that. It was one of the only things we differed on.

My guard was always up, and my ability to trust people, especially strangers from out of town, was limited. I was my brother's keeper. The first time I met Rico, I told Lorenzo I didn't trust him. There was something shifty in his eyes. They never matched the words that came out of his mouth or his emotions. He'd smile with his mouth, not his eyes, as if he were dead inside.

So, they tested the waters by hitting a few easy licks together to build trust. They had a good thing going for a short while, too, but a snake will always be a snake no matter how many times it sheds its skin. It didn't take long for Rico to learn the ins and outs of the drug operation my brother and his boys had built.

Rico's betrayal came out of nowhere. My heart dropped when I got the call. It was the nagging feeling in the pit of my stomach that I didn't want to be true. He'd set up my brother, sending him on a fake lick, which led to him being shot ten times and ending up in the hospital's intensive care unit.

Despite my pleas for God to take me instead, Lorenzo passed away on the third day, leaving an enormous hole in the center of my chest. Almost six months had passed since I lost him, and I still found myself reaching for the phone, ready to dial his number and hear his voice one more time.

As if shit couldn't go from bad to worse, I was diagnosed with TTP a few months after losing Lorenzo. The timing of it all felt like a cruel twist of fate, as if God was up there having one hell of a laugh at my expense. I wish I could say I felt sad or afraid when I first heard the news, but all I felt was relief. Like I was one step closer to being reunited with my brother again.

With a mother in a mental hospital that I'd only seen a handful of times and a sperm donor I'd never met, I had no other family or friends to turn to. The heaviness of my unexpected illness was overwhelming, to say the least, but a part of me looked at it as my karma for all the scamming and stealing I'd done over the years to make ends meet.

I missed my brother more than ever, knowing he would have been right by my side. I was grateful for XL unexpectedly stepping in and supporting me in his absence. That, plus receiving the treatments I needed, I was determined to fight for however many breaths I had left in me and honor the memory of the brother I lost.

THE NIGHT I WENT TO KILL RICO WAS THE NIGHT MY LIFE changed forever. I'd been scoping out his place and studying his routine for weeks, waiting for my chance to strike. One night, I did just that when I knew he'd be away from his apartment long enough for me to break inside and plant myself where he'd least expect it. I'd taken possession of Lorenzo's gun, ensuring it was filled with bullets. I intended to empty them all into Rico just like it had been done to my brother.

Once inside, I entered the master bedroom and stowed away in the back of the walk-in closet, waiting for him to come home. I stayed in the darkness of the closet for hours, the only light filtering from underneath the door. My resolve never wavered. I would wait all night if I had to. I wouldn't be happy until his blood was on my hands and his soul was eternally burning in Hell where it belonged.

My knees locked up, and my shoulders tensed when I heard the bedroom door open. My heart pounded so violently that I feared it would give my presence away. The moment I'd been waiting on had finally presented itself. Still, I couldn't move. It was like my feet had been rooted to the ground. Every creak of the floorboards on the other side of the door sent a zap of fear surging through me from the soles of my feet to my scalp. I tried holding my breath, praying it would make me feel as tiny and hushed as possible. The gun shook in my dominant hand as I reached for the closet door handle with my left. It was now or never.

Just as I went to turn the knob, I heard a scuffle on the other side of the door. Rico wasn't alone. The muffled sounds of the intruder and Rico knocking into his belongings felt like it would never end. I clutched my brother's gun, fingers trembling, praying I wouldn't be discovered. Suddenly, everything went silent, and I froze, refusing to believe it was over as quickly as it had started. The seconds stretched into infinity, each fleeting moment filled with alarm as I nervously reached for the knob again, curious to see the aftermath. The door swung open to my surprise, exposing me to a burly monster donned in all black. He had a mask over his face. All I could see was the soulless look in his eyes.

He took one look at the gun in my grasp and grumbled with displeasure. "Fuck. You're coming with me," he grunted before knocking the gun out of my hand and sending an elbow to the side of my head. I hit the ground, and everything went black.

I snapped out of my daze when there was a knock on the door. Doctor Ritter sailed inside. Instantly, my leg started shaking, and my heart galloped with angst as I awaited her news. My eyes bounced around my hospital room. The eggshell-painted walls were adorned with calming artwork of serene beaches and waterfalls. As beautiful as it was, it did little to soothe my bouncing nerves.

She greeted me with a kind, professional smile. "Good morning, Zahra. How are you feeling today?"

I straightened my posture in the bed. "Nervous but hopeful, I guess."

Dr. Ritter nodded, understanding my medical situation. Her nails tapped against the tablet nested in the crook of her left arm, seemingly pulling up my records. "I've reviewed your latest blood tests. The good news is everything looks stable. There's been no more damage to your red blood cells, and I feel comfortable discharging you today. However, you still need to continue to take your medication. I've already sent your prescription refills to the pharmacy."

My thoughts raced, trying to absorb the information quickly so I'd be ready for whatever came next. I felt a twist of anxiety coil tightly in my stomach. I was officially going back home to live with my husband. "Yes, I understand."

"Do you have someone who can drive you home?"

I nodded. "Yes. My, uh, husband can do it. He's been a big support system through this."

It had taken me over a month to sort out the paperwork and get me onto XL's insurance, let alone the time it took to start the daily treatments to remove the bad plasma from my blood and replace it with good plasma. I'd been in the hospital for weeks, receiving the treatments and recovering. He made sure to visit me every night, keeping me updated on everything going on outside the depressing hospital walls.

Dr. Ritter flashed a comforting smile. "That's great to hear. Having a solid support system makes a big difference. You have to want to fight to stay alive."

"I'm ready to do whatever it takes. I-I wanna fight. I wanna live."

Dr. Ritter leaned forward, a look of empathy in her brown eyes. "Good. I'll get to work on the discharge paperwork, and we'll see about getting you out of here as quickly as possible."

"Okay. Thank you, doctor."

"You're welcome."

As she left my room, a wave of emotions washed over me. Fear and determination swirled inside my head as I reached out to grab the phone XL had gotten me. He was the only number I had saved in my contacts. I couldn't help but think of him and how much he'd supported me through my hospital stay.

Hopefully, the plasma treatments continued to work. If not, I'd be facing down surgery. *And if that doesn't work, at least death will be quick and hopefully painless.* I knew the road ahead wouldn't be smooth, but with a good medical team and XL by my side, I felt a twinkle of hope I hadn't felt in a long time.

I EXITED THROUGH THE SLIDING HOSPITAL DOORS TO WAIT FOR XL to arrive, my mind preoccupied with thoughts about being alone with him in his apartment, amongst other things. I stepped onto the sidewalk, halting when a distant but recognizable female voice called my name.

"Zahra? Zahra Adams? Is that you?"

My neck slowly twisted around before the rest of my body followed. I saw Zyon Bennett, my former best friend from Miami, standing there, turning up her slim, pierced nose at me. The shock of seeing, let alone speaking to her after so many years, and in Vegas of all places, was clear as day in my expression.

Her burgundy box braids were pulled into a high bun, and her face was overly beaten with too much makeup and thick, mink lashes that hooded her cocoa-brown eyes. She wore a black business suit that hugged her slim-thick build, with a blush pink button-up shirt underneath that showed way too much cleavage. Between that and the three-inch peep-toe heels on her feet, it was giving professional whore, but I didn't bother to comment.

I arched an eyebrow before acknowledging her by name. "Zyon. I didn't expect to run into you here. It's been a minute."

She smirked before folding her arms across her busty chest. "Small world, huh? What brings you to Vegas? Trying to rewrite those ho facts from your past or just your reputation?"

My eyes narrowed slightly as a hint of annoyance crept into my voice. Seeing her again only brought up old feelings of resentment and hatred after what she did to my brother. It took everything in me not to call her out her name.

"Neither. I'm here visiting," I stated, refusing to go into detail about my health issues. "What about you? Moving on to another city to find a new nigga to betray?"

Zyon's forced smile tightened, but she didn't back down. Instead, she smacked her lips together. "Still holding a grudge, I see. That was high school, Zahra. Maybe it's time you let shit go and stopped living in the past."

I scoffed, crossing my arms in defense. "Funny coming from you, seeing as you were the one the bitch who couldn't even stay loyal to her best friend's brother and ran halfway across the country."

Her glare flashed with annoyance, but she kept her composure. "Trust, life's good over here, thanks for asking. It's called moving on. You should try that shit sometimes. It'll work wonders for your glow because, honestly, you lookin' blah."

I scoffed. "And how's shaking your ass for sweaty, balled-up dollar bills going for you? Or have you upgraded to a new scam these days?" I quizzed, referencing a rumor about her becoming a stripper once she moved out to Vegas to make ends meet.

The tension between us was apparent, two women both born and bred in Dade County standing our grounds, unwilling to show any sign of weakness and damn sure not backing down. There was a long, charged silence before Zyon finally broke it.

"If you must know, I just interviewed for a position here. I've got better shit to do than to waste my breath on you. Good luck with... whatever it is you're doing here."

With that, we parted ways, the unresolved drama still dangling. It was clear we both had our own shit going on. She didn't need to know about my failing health, and I didn't give a damn about her troubles. Running into Zyon after so long was a stinging reminder of her betrayal of my brother and our friendship.

I tried to shake off the encounter, focusing instead on XL as he rounded the corner, slowing the car as he looked for me.

My phone buzzed in my back pocket, and I answered without looking, knowing it was him. "Hey."

"Hey. I see you. I'm walking toward you."

"Stay where you are. I'll come to you," he instructed.

I stopped and allowed him to pull the car up to me. He put the car in park and got out to open the passenger side door for me and usher me inside. Once back behind the wheel, XL pulled off. We passed by Zyon, and the two of us traded evil glances. I didn't let my eyes leave hers until she was too far away for me to see anymore.

"So, how are you feeling today?" XL inquired, eyes darting away from the road to look at me. "You looked pissed as hell when I pulled up."

I eased out a calm breath, trying not to let my heartbeat go haywire at the thought of my back and forth with Zyon. "I'm good," I replied, shaking the devil off. "Happy to finally be out of there. You headed to the restaurant after you drop me off?"

"Yeah. You want me to bring you something home, or do you want me to cook tonight?"

I sighed, contemplating what I had a taste for. The thought of one of his soulful, home-cooked meals did sound appetizing, especially after the emotional roller coaster of the day I'd had. But before I could make up my mind, XL spoke up again.

"You know what, never mind. I'll cook something when I get back home. I've got a new recipe I've wanted to try anyway."

A slight smile tugged at my lips, feeling the tension in my nerves ease, knowing I had someone who cared. I appreciated his thoughtfulness. "Sounds good."

"Bet."

My mood had been slightly lifted by the anticipation of one of his comforting meals and his caring presence. I turned my gaze toward the window, vowing to let go of my negative encounter with Zyon and focus on the positive aspects of my life.

In the past three months we'd spent together, there'd been a silent transition from strangers to something more. Initially, it was a practical arrangement born out of necessity. XL stepped in and offered me a lifeline, and that was that. But the more I got to know him, the more I saw layers of his personality that intrigued me. He was protective, thoughtful, and surprisingly gentle for someone ready to put a bullet in my head the first night we met.

I loved how he listened intently when I talked about my health updates. I often looked forward to our late evenings together, the meals he cooked and brought over from the restaurant, and the quiet moments we shared in my hospital room. I could honestly say we were friends. It was a big difference to the withdrawn life I'd grown accustomed to since Lorenzo passed. It was surprisingly as natural as breathing. XL's ability to juggle all the different aspects of his busy life and still make me feel seen and valued without the added intimacy of sex had managed to win me over in ways I didn't expect.

But telling him I was beginning to feel things friends shouldn't feel for each other would ruin everything. Wouldn't it?

XI

I walked into the apartment with the aroma of garlic and spices wafting past my nose from the ingredients in my shopping bag. I'd been experimenting with a new soul food recipe and wanted to add a healthy side salad to the meal—a habit I'd picked up thanks to Zahra's influence. Unbeknownst to her, she'd encouraged me to change some of my eating habits. I'd lost about ten pounds since Zahra started nudging me toward healthier choices, and I felt better for it.

I set the bag down on the counter in the kitchen, washed my hands, and quickly got to work. My skilled hands moved with ease as I prepped the ingredients and preheated the oven. As I chopped up the fresh vegetables for the salad, my thoughts drifted to Amir and Nerissa's upcoming wedding.

I heard the bedroom door swing open from down the hall and followed the sound of light footsteps until Zahra appeared in the kitchen. She drew a deep breath, inhaling the rich, savory scents of the soul food filling the room. She flashed me a grin, clearly a sign of preapproval for the meal.

"Yum, cucumbers," she said, stealing one from the cutting board and crunching it between her perfectly aligned teeth.

I smirked. "With all this healthy eating, I've slimmed down ten pounds. I'm gonna look good as hell in that tux at Amir's wedding this weekend," I boasted.

She chuckled with a playful look in her eyes. "Yeah. I'm sure you'll turn more heads than the blushing bride."

I grinned, enjoying our light-hearted banter. "Yo, you should come with me," I blurted out.

I looked up just in time to see Zahra's smile falter slightly before she shook her head.

"You know I'm supposed to be a ghost when it comes to your family. That's what we agreed on. It's too risky."

I put the knife down and stepped closer, my tone reassuring. "Too many people will be there. You'll blend in. Just sit in the back and have a good time. You deserve to leave the house, especially now that you're out of the hospital."

"I'm not a recluse."

"Bullshit," I replied, calling her bluff. "C'mon, we can pretend that you're a distant cousin on the bride's side, and I'll be the handsome groomsman trying not to overshadow the bride and groom with all my fineness."

She smirked at my joke. "That sounds like something straight out of a fiction book."

"You'd read it, though, right?"

Zahra chuckled, though she still looked visibly torn. "From cover to cover." She'd been so focused on her health, never leaving the hospital, that she hadn't allowed herself to think past the hospital walls. "Alright, I'll go. But only because you've convinced me that it'll be the biggest mistake of my life not to see you in that tux."

My face lit up as contentment hooked my mouth. "Bet. Now, let me get back to work. I promise this will be worth it."

Forty-five minutes later, we sat at the table, and I put her plate in front of her. Zahra took a bite of everything—the Cajun seasoned, pan-seared salmon, red-skinned potatoes with shrimp and crab, and kale salad, her eyes widening as her tastebuds danced in delight.

"Oh shit, this is amazing! You've outdone yourself," she said between bites.

A surge of pride washed over me as I cheesed. "Thanks. I'm glad you like it. I lied about wanting to add this to the menu. This is actually the dinner for my cousin Amir's wedding this weekend. My restaurant is catering."

"I'm sure all the guests will love it."

"Yeah. Me too."

Zahra sighed and set her fork down on the edge of her plate. "While we're back on the wedding topic, what if I can't find anything to wear? It's not like I have a closet overflowing with clothes here. And then there's this..." she said, her voice trailing off as she nervously rubbed the fading flat, red spots and bruises on her arms.

I swung my head in a no, refusing to let her self-esteem fall in my presence. "What spots, Zahra? Everything is practically gone. And besides, it's been three months. You don't have to hide it from me anymore."

"I might not have it hide it from you, but I don't want to wear anything with my arms out for the wedding. I've been so self-conscious about them for so long that it's just hard to reprogram my brain to think otherwise. I want to blend in just like you said."

"Trust me, you have no reason to be self-conscious. You could put on anything and look good."

She smiled shyly. "Thanks."

"If you're feeling up to it, we'll hit some stores tomorrow and see if we can find something that makes you comfortable. Sound good?"

Zahra nodded with a warm grin spreading across her face. "Yeah. It does."

Zahra

The wedding venue was the beautiful Bellagio Conservatory and Botanical Gardens. It was filled with hundreds of preserved roses, blooming orchids, shrubs, and trees. The beautiful aroma of the blooming flowers alone added a touch of magic to the space. I took my seat in the back as planned, in awe of the enchanting scene. The ceremony was minutes away from beginning, and the butterflies in the pit of my stomach still hadn't seemed to disappear.

Getting dressed for the wedding had been more of a challenge than I anticipated. I'd been feeling self-conscious about the faded bruises and red spots on my arm from my health condition, and I wanted to find something that would make me feel beautiful and comfortable when I put it on. After a full day of dragging XL around the city looking for something to wear, I finally found the perfect dress—a simple, long-sleeved, black satin dress that hugged my curves and flowed down to my knees.

The dress had a subtle shimmer that caught the light just right. The long sleeves provided the coverage I needed, while the sleek black color complemented my skin tone and made me feel like I'd blend in with the other guests perfectly. The last thing I wanted to be was the center of attention on someone else's big day. I paired it with gold chandelier earrings, a pendant necklace, and strappy black heels. My hair was styled in long, loose waves that cascaded over my shoulders, and my soft glam makeup, with a hint of Fenty highlighter and a glossy lip, completed my look.

As the music started and the bridal party started to trickle in, I couldn't help but feel overjoyed for the two people about to join together in holy matrimony, and I'd never met either of them. I stood to my feet as the bride descended the aisle. My breath caught in my throat. She looked breathtaking in her flowing ivory gown. Her perfectly beat face radiated nothing but love. Her teary eyes were stationed on the groom, who stood at the altar with a fresh haircut and a look of genuine awe. The love they shared was glaring, filling the entire space with a warmth I knew everyone felt right along with me.

As stunning as she was, my attention quickly shifted to the groomsman standing next to the best man—XL. He looked so damn good in his tailored tux, just like he said he would. He stood tall and proud, his eyes occasionally glancing over at me with a playful smirk. Seeing him standing up there, looking handsome and proud, I felt more at ease. His almond-shaped, mahogany-brown eyes and attractive smile reassured me that everything was perfect. I knew that he saw me and not my condition.

Damn. He does look amazing up there.

His rich chocolate skin, wide-set nose, and full lips were all buttery smooth. His hair was freshly cut with a crisp edge up, and the low curls on the top of his head perfectly gelled. The goatee and thick, desirable beard wrapped from ear to ear were perfectly trimmed, and his ears and neck were dripping in gold—a thick Cuban link chain and earrings filled with diamonds.

Throughout the ceremony, I couldn't stop my eyes from floating back to XL. I studied him as he listened intently to the vows, bowed his head during prayer, and softened his expression with emotion when the soloist sang "Here and Now" by Luther Vandross. He was everything I admired in a black man—handsome, Herculean, protective, and genuine. And seeing him standing there, part of such a special moment, only made me grow fonder of him.

Dating in Miami was nearly impossible. And by nearly, I mean entirely. Any man I dealt with that had a three-zero-five area code had *always* been a scammer, cheater, lacked basic manners, or pretended to have money while selling other niggas fake Patek watches.

After years of back-to-back bad dates, sex, and relationships, I quit altogether. I was tired of trying to weed through all the scamming ass niggas with empty pockets, toxic masculinity, mommy, and commitment issues. Miami wasn't the city to find love, especially if you were someone who demanded basic respect, didn't play games, set their standards higher than a giraffe's neck, and sought out a long-term relationship with a nigga who knew how to be loyal. It wasn't up for debate.

No wonder half the females out there were OnlyFans models or on their city girl shit trying to get their hustle on the best way they knew how. Nothing in Miami was real. Why should feelings be? That's why it was so easy for me to say yes to marrying XL in the first place. The last thing I expected after being closed off for so long was for my heart to soften toward a nigga that had a gun pointed to my face during our initial encounter.

As the couple exchanged their rings, I couldn't help but think about my "wedding" and how it didn't mirror anything unfolding before me. It was almost laughable. Wearing the clothes he'd kidnapped me in, XL and I walked into a small wedding chapel with a neon "Wedding Chapel" sign. Inside, the pungent odor of cigarette smoke hit me as soon as we entered. There was a row of loud clanking slot machines, six fancy red velvet pews where other couples looked on, and a janky arch with fake flowers wrapped around it. We trekked down the aisle lined with silk rose petals, greeted by an officiant wearing a gold Elvis Presley suit that was two sizes too small. He led us through the speedy ceremony.

Our standard vow exchange captured the spontaneity of our unplanned decision to marry. Still, when we locked eyes, we knew we were committed to seeing where the journey would take us, at least in the meantime. He pronounced us husband and wife, and the onlookers clapped, one offering to snap a picture of us on my phone to capture the memorable moment. That was it. No dress. No bouquet. No rings. No kiss. Just us, Elvis, and a few strangers we'd never see again. We'd never know what it felt like to look at each other the way his cousin and his bride were. We were nothing but a scam.

AFTER THE CEREMONY, EVERYONE MOVED TO A SPACE FOR cocktail hour, beautifully decorated with more extravagant floral arrangements and twinkling lights. XL made his way through the crowd, approaching me showing a full grid of his white teeth and a sparkle in his eyes that made my heart stumble out a frantic beat.

"You enjoying yourself?" he asked before pulling me into a tight hug. "Damn, you smellin' all good and shit."

I worked up a cocky grin, feeling all the feels. "Thank you. And yes, it was such a beautiful ceremony. And you looked handsome up there."

He chuckled. "Thanks. I couldn't take my eyes off you, either. You look perfect. Don't you ever let a nigga tell you otherwise. That dress looks damn good on you."

"Thanks. You remember how nervous I was about what to wear, but I think I pulled it off," I stated, looking down at my dress as if I didn't already know what I had on.

"I told you you'd look amazing."

"Takes one to know one. No more XL for you. People gon' have to start calling you Large," I joked, keeping the mood light.

He laughed with me. "Oh, you got jokes, huh?"

"Just a little. But seriously, thank you for inviting me and making me get out of the house. I think I'm going to go outside and call an Uber."

"You sure you gotta go?"

"Yeah. A ceremony is one thing, but a reception where people's names are on assigned seats is another. I'm not trying to ruin a good thing."

He nodded. "You're right. I'm glad you and that dress made it off the hanger and out the house."

I blushed, tearing my eyes down to my heels. "You just make sure to sneak me a piece of cake before you leave, all right?"

XL smirked. "I got you."

"I'm just going to make a quick trip to the bathroom, and then I'll be out of here. Enjoy the rest of your night, and I'll see you back home later."

"Thanks. I will."

I stepped out of the bathroom stall, adjusting my dress as I headed to the sink to wash my hands. As I approached, I noticed a pregnant woman in a flowy, dusty pink dress standing there. Our eyes locked in the mirror, and I paused, frozen in shock. We recognized each other instantly. *Sienna? What the hell is she doing here? Was she a part of the wedding?*

If she were, I hadn't noticed her standing up there during the ceremony since I sat in the back, too focused on how good XL looked to see anyone else. Trying to compose myself, I approached the sink beside her and washed my hands as usual.

"Zahra? What are you doing out here?" Her voice sounded surprised and confused.

I kept my eyes on her reflection while trying to keep my voice steady. "I'm not here. You never saw me."

But she wasn't convinced. She grabbed my wrist when I reached for a paper towel, her grip firm. "What? What do you mean?"

I snatched my wrist away, my heart bucking all out of rhythm. It wasn't the time or place for explanations.

"Seriously, Sienna. I can't talk right now. Just promise me you won't say anything to anyone, okay? You never saw me."

Her eyes popped wide, filled with suspicion, as her brows dipped low. "Why the hell not?"

I took a deep breath, knowing I had to make her understand the gravity of the situation one way or another. "Because I'm supposed to be dead!" I hissed.

Her mouth fell open in shock, and I could see the questions forming on her lips, ready to fall right off her tongue. But I couldn't risk staying to answer them. Panic surged through me like a bucking bronco, and I rushed out of the bathroom, hands still dripping wet and my mind racing.

I headed for the exit, feeling spooked. *First Zyon, then Sienna. Fuck.* My unexpected encounter with Sienna had shaken me to my core. I was almost to the door when I saw XL approaching. He caught my swinging arm gently. Concern was etched into his expression.

"Yo, slow down. Where are you going, flying out of here like a bat out of hell? You good?"

I forced a stiff smile, barely able to hide my anxiety. "I'm good. I'm just tired, and my Uber is about to pull up."

XL looked at me, his eyes searching for the truth. "You sure you straight?"

I nodded. I had genuinely enjoyed the wedding despite my recent bathroom run-in with a blast from my past. "Yeah, I am."

He conceded a smile, but I could tell he was still worried. "You sure it's just that you're tired?"

I didn't want to let on that I knew Sienna from our Miami days and that our meeting had rattled the hell out of me. I prayed she would keep quiet and not say anything about seeing me. If I had the power to, I'd completely erase myself from her mind.

"Mmhm, I'm just tired. I'll see you back at home, okay? And don't forget my cake!"

XL dipped his chin, though he still hadn't been able to shake the look of uncertainty on his face. "Yeah, all right. I got you. Get some rest. I'll see you later." Just as I was about to leave, his phone vibrated. He glanced at the screen, his expression changing from unease to alarm. "Hold up a second. It's the alarm company. Hello? What? Fuck! I'm on my way! I'm on my way right now!" he yelled into the receiver before ending the call.

"What happened?" I asked, my heart racing in a panic.

"My barbershop is on fire."

My heart sank as I watched the distress wash over his face. I knew how much his barbershop meant to him. At that moment, I pushed my own selfish worries to the backburner and focused entirely on him.

"Oh my God. You need to go. Get there as soon as you can!"

XL nodded, already moving toward the exit. He rushed to his car, the situation's urgency pushing all other thoughts aside. As he disappeared, I couldn't help but pray that everything would be okay for his business and between me and Sienna.

XI

As I sped away from the venue, a million thoughts raced through my head, all bringing worry and anger along with them. With her being so tired, I didn't feel right letting Zahra catch an Uber home, but I knew she needed to get there safely, and I couldn't be the one to do it. The thought of my barbershop, my first business, going up in flames filled me with a mix of dread and fury I hadn't felt since we lost Big Mama.

When I arrived at the scene, the traumatic sight before me was enough to make a weak nigga's knees buckle. Fire trucks lined the street, flashing red and white lights and casting an unnerving glow against the pavement. Firefighters worked tirelessly, hoses spraying gallons of water at the flames that engulfed my barbershop. The night air was thick with smoke, and the smell of burning wood and chemicals stung my eyes and nostrils so severely that I had to shield my face with one hand and wave away smoke with the other.

I took off my suit jacket, ready to step forward and help fight the flames, when I felt a hand grip my shoulder. I turned to see Ahsan and Amir standing behind me. I called them from the car to inform them of the fire since I'd left without saying a word to anyone but

Zahra. They both insisted on coming, despite my initial protests about them staying and enjoying the wedding festivities, especially Amir. I didn't want my stumbling block to sour his special day. Still, their presence was a small comfort amid my whole world going up in flames, literally.

Hate pooled in my stomach like acid. "I can't believe this shit is happening," I mumbled, staring at the blaze swallowing up my building.

Ahsan looked surly as he surveyed the scene. "We'll get to the bottom of this shit, man. I promise you that. You know we got you."

Amir, always the more emotional one since he was the baby, clenched his fists in frustration. "Who the fuck would do some shit like this? This place meant everything to you!"

"It meant everything to a lot of people," I said, thinking about my regulars—the clients, both local and famous alike, who'd been coming in faithfully since my doors opened, as well as my freelance barbers and employees.

Over the years, they'd become somewhat like family. Where would they go? My heart dropped half a foot as I thought about the countless hours, the sweat, and the dreams I'd poured into that shop. Watching it all burn to the ground made my stomach sour.

I swiped my hand over my beard, tearing my eyes away from the blaze long enough to trade glances with Amir. "You shouldn't even be here right now, nigga. It's your fucking wedding day. Get back to your bride! I'll be straight."

"Nerissa damn near pushed me out the door to be here for you. I'm good right where I'm at. Besides, the guests are eating anyway, so we have time."

"Sienna is good too. We're focused on you right now, nigga," Ahsan assured me.

We stood there watching the firefighters work to bring the blaze under control. But the damage had already been done. It was more than just an attack on my business; it was a declaration of war toward our family and everything we'd worked so hard to build. A police officer approached our huddle with a serious expression.

"Are any of you the owners of this establishment?"

"I am," I announced, stepping forward. "I'm Kendrick Patton."

"Hi, Mr. Patton. I'm Officer Doug Reynolds. I'm sorry this happened."

"Do you have any leads? Any details as to how the fire started in the first place?"

"Everything is still under investigation, but by the looks of things, we have reason to believe this was arson."

Ahsan stepped forward, his tone demanding answers. "Arson? What makes you think it was arson?"

Officer Reynolds nodded, pulling out a notepad. "We found a gasoline can in a dumpster a few blocks down, which indicates that the fire could've been set intentionally. Once the fire marshal declares it's okay for us to go inside, we'll have our investigators do chemical testing to detect gasoline inside. We've also recovered what fingerprints we could from the gas can."

"And what's being done in the meantime? We're just supposed to sit here and twiddle our damn thumbs?" Amir added.

As badly as I wanted to speak, my cousins beat me to the punch at every turn. A surge of anger and helplessness spread like ice through my insides. My business, my livelihood, was destroyed, and it was clear it was likely a deliberate act.

"We're checking the traffic cameras in the area for any signs of who did this. We'll follow up with you once we have more information."

I clenched my fists. "I don't understand why the fuck someone would do this!"

Officer Reynolds gave me a sympathetic look. "We'll do everything we can to find out exactly what happened. In the meantime, I suggest you start thinking about what you'll need to file an insurance claim and start to rebuild."

I scoffed. *As if it were that simple.* I stood there, feeling mixed emotions—outrage, brokenhearted, and only a pinch of grit. My cousins remained by my side. Their support was a tangible reminder that I wasn't alone, no matter how alienated I felt.

"We'll rebuild on my land," Ahsan confirmed, speaking it into existence. "Anything you want, anywhere you want it. No matter what it takes."

He and his brother nodded in agreement as if the decision was final, standing firm in their loyalty.

"You fuckin' right we will, nigga. We're family, and Patton boys stick together," Amir confirmed.

Officer Reynolds stepped off as the barbershop smoldered, a painful reminder of the permanent destruction. I swore I'd find out who was behind the fire and ensure they paid for what they did. But in the meantime, I had to focus on picking up the charred pieces of the dream I'd worked so hard to create from scratch and starting over.

I looked at my cousins, both visibly as disturbed as I was. "We haven't made any new enemies lately, have we?"

Ahsan crossed his arms, his expression tense like he was trying to pass a hard turd. "I thought all of our loose ends were tied. Nothing should've led to this kind of attack. Whoever did this had better be ready to start a fuckin' war."

Amir shook his head, frustration evident in his baritone voice. "It doesn't make any goddamn sense. I've been keeping things low-key with the business. Who the fuck would want to go this far?"

I considered his words, feeling a vein pulsing over my temple. "Maybe it's somebody we didn't see coming. Somebody lurking in the shadows, holding a grudge we didn't know about."

"But who?" Amir grumbled. "There's no Bradley. No Jules. No Demario. No fuckin' bitch ass Rico."

I rolled my thick shoulder in a shrug. "I don't know, but we need to figure out who and why."

Ahsan's eyes scanned the scene as he spoke. "You don't think this is somehow tied to the vandalization of Sienna's work at the art gallery, do you?"

I paused, trying to piece together what minimal clues we had. "What does Sienna's art have to do with my shop?"

Amir grunted. "Yeah. I'm not seeing the connection either."

"They could be someone new trying to make a name for themselves. Or maybe it's personal. Someone with a personal vendetta against you or the business itself. Have you fired anybody recently? Anybody come in with a complaint?" Ahsan questioned.

I swung my head. "Nah. Nothing like that. This shit came out of left fuckin' field."

"You don't think it's Cannon, do you?" Amir insinuated. "The mothafucka did just get out, and he's fucking with Brandi now."

Ahsan scoffed. "The only thing that should be on a nigga's mind who been on lockdown as long as he was should be P-U-S-S-Y and nothin' but."

Amir sighed, rubbing the back of his neck. "Yeah, well. You know how stupid niggas can be. And Brandi is the fuckin' queen of Petty-Land. I wouldn't put shit past her."

"I think we should keep all our options open and dig deeper. Let's look into recent conflicts or anyone with a reason to target XL."

I nodded, appreciating their insight and assistance. "I agree. I'll have to tell the other barbers and employees about the fire anyway, so I'll check in with them. They might have noticed something I didn't," I stated.

Ahsan grunted. "Talk to everyone, review security footage, and let us know if the police find anything on the traffic cameras. We're not going to let this shit slide. Nobody fucks with us and gets away with it."

Amir clapped a hand on my shoulder, his grip firm. "Whoever did this will regret fuckin' with us, and that's on God and everything I love."

I nodded in agreement, my determination clear. "When I find out who's behind this, I'll make sure they burn to fuckin' ashes just like my building did."

It was late when I finally walked through the door to my spacious two-bedroom apartment. The night's events had gone from joy and love to heartbreak and thoughts of violence. To my surprise and relief, Zahra was still up and waiting for me. As soon as she saw me, she got up from the couch, still wearing the dress that made my dick throb. *Down, boy.*

She approached, her eyes were filled with concern.

"What the hell happened? I've been so worried. I paced this floor until my feet got tired."

I shook my head, not ready to relive the nightmare of the fire just yet. Plus, I still had more questions than answers, and I didn't like that shit. "I appreciate you waiting up for me, but I really don't want to talk about it right now."

But Zahra wouldn't take no for an answer. She reached out and took my hand, her touch gentle and reassuring. We'd touched before on some friendly shit—a hug or quick handhold here and there, but this felt... different.

"I know your head and heart are probably going to war right now. I don't know what it feels like to lose a business, but I do know loss. I'm right here for you. Just like you've been there for me through my health struggles, all right? Let's sit down on the couch and talk. Say whatever you want. I'll be your sounding board."

We moved to the couch, and I reluctantly dropped my tired bones down next to her. The comfort of her presence was undeniable, but the pain and anger still simmering beneath the surface made me want to keep my distance. She waited patiently, holding space for me to find my words.

"The police think it's arson. No leads yet, though," I said, finally.

Her long, faux lashes flew high with shock. "Arson? Like somebody did it intentionally?"

"Yeah."

"Do you have any enemies? Anyone who might want to hurt you or the shop?"

I rubbed my temples, the stress of the situation physically taking its toll on my body. "At this point, it could be fuckin' anybody. The whole ride home, I couldn't help but think, what if this is retaliation for what happened to Rico... or somebody tied to you."

She considered my words, her expression upset. "I thought you said no one saw you take us from Miami."

"I'm too much of a boss not to be thorough. We took extra precautions to make sure we weren't followed."

"Okay, well, my brother is dead. I don't have any close friends, my mother's in a mental hospital, and I don't speak to the few other distant family members I do have. No one would be coming after you to get to me because the only person who gives a fuck about me is you."

I felt the weight of my frustration and helplessness pressing down on me. Fuck. I didn't mean to make her think I was somehow blaming her for the fire. That was the last thing I wanted to do. A soft sigh escaped my lips. "I'm sorry. I'm grasping at straws like everyone else right now."

Zahra's eyes softened, and she gently guided me to lay my head on her lap. "I'm so sorry this happened to you. Come here. It's been a day, and you need to rest."

I hesitated for a moment before giving in. The smooth velvet fabric of her dress felt like heaven against my skin. As I lay on her lap, her nurturing fingertips began to stroke my waves soothingly. Every beat of my heart reminded me of the fractures in my soul. The splinters had spread through me like a virus, but Zahra was the antidote. Her gentle touch was calming, providing solace to my tattered nerves. Despite the anger and mayhem bottled up inside me, something about her presence brought me a measure of peace I didn't think I'd be able to feel given the circumstances. She grounded me, and I didn't know what I'd do without her. I sat up slowly, wanting to look at her right side up. She shied away from my gaze.

"Look at me," I commanded. It was gentle but carried an edge that made her spine straighten.

Our eyes locked, and I saw raw and unmasked hunger behind her eyes. It also stirred something primal in me, a dark craving that twisted in my belly with a life of its own.

"XL…" she started, the words tangling with the knots of desire and fear bouncing around inside us both.

"Shh." I hushed her with a finger against her lips. "Don't."

"We shouldn't. Not when you're feeling this bad," she whispered, the truth of the matter laced with a yearning she couldn't conceal.

Her innocent words didn't match the savagery in her eyes. It drew me in like a moth to a flame, knowing full well the danger of the burn. "Bad doesn't even scratch the mothafuckin surface," I replied, my voice a low rumble that vibrated through my bones. "When I'm like this, I'm a niggas' worst kind of nightmare."

"You say that like I should be afraid," she said, recklessly moving closer.

Her eyes darkened. The awful promise within them sent an icy chill down my spine, even with all the heat between us.

"Zahra, I'll break you. You know that, right?" My hands cupped her face, thumbs brushing her soft cheeks with a tenderness that made me almost forget my threat.

"What if I'm already broken?" she countered, her breath hitching as my gaze bore into hers. The terrible beauty of her stormy brown eyes held me captive, and I leaned into her without hesitation.

"Not by me," I replied. There was a challenge in my tone, a dare that I found impossible not to wager.

"Not yet," she breathed out, sealing her fate with those two simple words.

Because despite every rational thought, every whisper of self-preservation when it came to my heart, I knew she craved the destruction I promised, the annihilation of her pussy only I could deliver.

"Fuck," I muttered, and for a moment, I felt the conflict between my heart and my head before my expression settled into a mask of hardened resolve. "You have no idea what you're asking for."

"Then show me," she challenged, closing the gap between us until our bodies aligned in a perfect, dangerous harmony.

My lips crashed against hers, a collision of need and inevitability, and the world disappeared. It was just us, broken pieces finding solace, a storm of passion threatening to sweep us both under.

"Remember you asked for this," I grumbled against her mouth as my hands gripped her hips with a possessiveness that left no room for doubt.

Zahra was mine in this life and the next.

"Remember I said yes," she shot back.

The last fragment of my restraint crumbled to dust. This was it. This was real. There was no going back once we crossed the line. And nothing would ever be the same between us again. I lifted her into my arms as if she weighed nothing. My strides were sure and steady despite the shadows dancing in the hallway's corners. In seconds, the warmth of my bed enveloped her. She pulled me close. The warmth of her body was a welcomed variation to the cold that had seeped deep into my bones.

"Kendrick," she managed to say, her voice no more than a breath as her fingers found the hem of my dress shirt, tugging me closer. I stiffened for a moment. Shock or maybe hesitation flickered across my features. But she didn't stop. We both wanted, no, *needed,* this connection. The feel of her tattooed thighs under my strong hands made me crave more of the sensual yet savage aura she exuded.

I flipped her over, and she straddled me in the darkness, feeling me beneath her, thick and hard enough to bust through concrete. My hand slid over her curves, pushing up the hem of her dress as she pushed her hands down past the barrier of my waistband, eliciting a hiss from between my clenched teeth. Immediately, I knew touching her was a bad idea. Once I started, it would be impossible to stop.

"Zahra," I called out, clenching my hand over her wrist. I wanted to tell her she was right—we shouldn't take things any further or cross the line and consummate our marriage. I wanted to say no, but I couldn't deny myself any longer.

"Shh," she urged, her whisper a defiant growl. "I know what you've shown me. What you think you are. But I'm ready to see you. All of you."

"Zahra," I said again.

My protest was weak, and my body betrayed me as I responded to her touch. My breath hitched. My dick was hard beneath her hand, beefy and strong as the blood pumped through it.

"Tell me you don't want this," she said, cutting me off. "Tell me, and I'll stop."

I couldn't say that. I wanted her too damn bad, and the hunger in her eyes told me we were both dangerously close to the edge of something neither of us could walk away from.

"Fuck." I cursed softly as my eyes locked onto hers, full of a tumultuous need that matched the chaos of my night.

A smirk played on her lips when she realized the sweet control she had over me. "Thought so."

"Zahra, this, *us*, it's madness," I murmured against her soft lips, a last-ditch attempt at holding onto my sanity.

"Then let's be mad together."

Her sweet lips captured mine, deading the possibility of any more words flying out and letting the world burn around us as we drowned in each other. The room's air was heavy with tension. I couldn't tear my gaze away from Zahra's beauty as the silvery moonlight cast shadows across her petite body that tensed beneath my touch.

"But I do need all of you tonight. Don't make me wait anymore." Her voice was breathless, pleading, as she pressed her body against mine, feeling every ridge and plane of muscle through the thin fabric of my shirt.

"Zahra, this is crazy," I groaned, but my voice had no conviction, only a raw edge of longing.

"Then let's be crazy together," she whispered back as her hand found the top of my dress slacks and tugged at the button, desperate to free me and feel me deep inside her.

"Fuck, Zahra." I cursed under my breath when her fingers finally managed to work my trousers open. My restraint was slipping, and it only fueled her urgency.

She slid down my body, her lips trailing a path over my exposed, tatted brown chest. I was hot to the touch, every inch pulsing with a fierce energy that matched my fury. Zahra wrapped her full, soft lips around the tip of my dick, and a deep, guttural moan escaped from my lips that sent shivers down my spine.

"If it makes you feel better to suck my dick, to take what you want, then take all of me, woman. Take every last drop," I rasped out, my words barely audible above the roar of my thumping heart.

She took my words as a challenge, taking me deeper into her mouth and letting the taste of my dick fill her senses.

"Mmm, shit. Yeah. Just like that," I hissed as my hands tangled in her hair, guiding her with an urgency that mirrored my need. Each stroke of her mouth was like a silent vow to make me lose all control, to have me break even more apart, only to piece ourselves back together in the aftermath.

"Fuck, Zahra, I..." My words cut off into a sharp intake of breath as she moved away, consumed by the feeling.

Our heavy breathing nearly drowned out the ripping of the fabric on the dress I liked so much, but it was the loudest sound to my ears as the torn sleeve slipped from her shoulder. Zahra let her dress, bra, and lace thong pool at her feet. My gaze, heavy with want, scorched her bare flesh as I studied each curve of her body.

"Come here," I demanded, my voice rough like sandpaper.

She climbed back on top of me, and every line of my muscular body tensed beneath her. Without hesitation, she brought one of her plump breasts to my lips. The sensation of her hard nipple in my mouth, drawing her in deeply, only made my dick pulsate harder. It was an erasure of all the jagged memories of the night that tried to claw their way back into my mind. My hands were on her body like a tattoo, my mouth was on her, and nothing could touch us, not the past, not the pain, and definitely not my enemies.

"I wanna be inside you so bad," I confessed in a tortured whisper between mouthfuls of her skin. She tore my shirt away, leaving me to absorb the warmth of her silky skin.

"Then don't stop," she breathed out, her voice steady even as her body trembled with need. "You're the only man I want inside me ever again."

An answering groan vibrated through me as she rolled her hips against me, teasing both of us with the promise of what was to come. My dick was hard, and the heat and force of her sliding back and forth against me, not yet claiming each other but promising everything, had me ready to explode.

She moaned softly. "Fuck, it feels so good."

"You ain't seen nothin' yet. I'm going to eat that pussy and watch my dick stretch you open, baby. I'm going to watch it all," I promised as my hand gripped her hair and pulled her down for a kiss that stole my breath straight from my lungs.

"Show me now," she challenged, her voice laced with desire as she rose so that I could pull down my trousers and boxers to my ankles.

I had a wicked smile on my face as I stepped forward again, my erection leading the way. Our bodies were almost touching, and she squeezed her thighs together.

"Mmm. I can't wait to devour this pussy," I whispered. I didn't sound controlling when I said the words. It sounded more like a confession.

The heat in the room was rising fast. I pulled her to the edge of the bed before dropping to my knees in front of her, ready to devour her as if she were my last meal. I knew she was still insecure about the marks on her skin, and I made sure to kiss them all before dropping my head between her thighs and sliding my tongue up her sweet core.

Her body instantly shook with pleasure as I suckled on her

enlarged clit like the tip of a fresh strawberry. I was a big nigga. And big niggas liked to eat, both food and pussy alike. I had no doubt that my tongue game would keep her pussy bussin' like an AK.

"I've been thinking about this all day. Ever since I saw you in that fuckin' dress," I professed from between her thighs.

She cried out my name as she rolled her hips against my long, thick tongue. I pushed two fingers inside her warmth while circling my tongue around her needy, wet spot. It didn't take long for her orgasm to surface. My tongue game was that venomous. I ate pussy almost as good as I threw down in the kitchen.

"Oooh shit! I'm cumming!" she squealed as her body twitched and her thighs tensed on both sides of my head.

She rode out her climax until her body fell limp, and I lapped her pussy clean like a fat kid with a chocolate ice cream cone.

"I'm selfish. I don't share."

I could've stopped there. I was ready to. I wanted to respect the fact that she tired quickly. As badly as I wanted to put her beautiful ass through the mattress, I was good with the fact that she'd gotten hers.

"XL, please," she whined, her limbs heavy and limp.

"Tell me what you want, Zahra."

"You. Inside me. Now."

"You're a woman after my own heart." I pushed her legs further apart and dragged two fingers up and down her core. "I could get used to this."

I lay beside her, and Zahra positioned herself above me. With a deep, soul-satisfying groan, she sank onto me, taking every inch of my dick fully inside her. The fit was tight and perfect as if we were two puzzle pieces clicking together after a lifetime of being misplaced. She started to move, finding a rhythm with me that had my king-sized bed creaking and our mingled gasps filling the room.

"Mmm, fuck," she moaned into my mouth.

The sweet taste of her lips, the feel of her on top of me, the way my dick filled her tight pussy right up, it was all-consuming, and I *never* wanted it to end. I groaned against her mouth as her hands roamed over my tatted chest with a hunger she couldn't contain. Her touch was fiery against my skin, igniting every nerve ending in a blaze of need.

My free hand caught hers, guiding it down her trembling abdomen to the place where I knew she needed me most. Zahra circled her clit with her middle finger, needing that extra little push, just the right amount of pleasure to tip her over the edge.

I groaned. "Cum for me, baby. Please cum for me."

The raw edge in my voice made her nipples harden even more. My hand gripped her hair, not painfully, just enough to tilt her head back and claim her lips again in a searing kiss that spoke of possessiveness and an insatiable craving.

My command unraveled her further, pushing her toward the cliff she was so desperate to tumble over. Zahra circled her clit with fervent urgency, the slick heat of her body betraying how close she was to shattering into a million pieces of ecstasy.

"Fuck, I-I'm... c-cumming!" The words lodged in her throat as a loud gasp tore through her, unbidden and wild. I'd found the sweet spot on her neck, my teeth sinking in just enough to send her spiraling. Her inner walls clenched around me, fierce and demanding as her back arched, pressing her C-cup breasts flush against my inked chest.

Zahra convulsed, helpless in the wake of another orgasm that swept away every fractured part of her, leaving only the woman who was whole when she was in my arms and nothing else.

Switching positions, Zahra got on all fours. I was nearing my climax and didn't want our time together to end. I threw the thoughts from my mind and wrapped my hands around her waist, inserting every inch of my long, thick dick inside her honeypot.

Zahra moaned. "Fuck, you make me feel so good."

I slowly pushed in and out. "Yeah. Tell daddy how good."

"Mm, fuck. So good. Faster."

"Are you sure?" I confirmed while gripping her hips tighter.

"So sure. I wanna feel you in my stomach."

She lifted to her knees, and I snaked my arm around her, squeezing her right breast as her spine pressed into my chest. She laced her fingers over mine, demanding every ounce of stamina I had left. I took it as a personal challenge to fuck her goddamn brains out. Zahra twisted her neck toward me, and I mashed my lips against hers. Our tongues tangled as I fucked her harder, moving faster in and out.

"Kendrick," she whimpered, feeling me move behind her, a testament to our power over each other. My name had become a mantra, a prayer, a curse, all wrapped up in how I made her body feel.

The world faded to a blur, leaving only the rhythm of Zahra's body colliding with mine. My breath was hot on her skin, my gasps matching the erratic beat of her heart.

"Zahra," I groaned, feeling the vibration of her against my flesh. It was guttural and laced with a raw need that resonated deeply within me—something words hadn't been invented to explain yet.

"Say it again, baby," she demanded, her voice barely above a whisper as she pushed back against me, finding a rhythm that was frantic and perfectly in sync.

"Zahra," I repeated, each syllable punctuated by my thrusts, driving up into her as if I sought redemption at the core of her being. And maybe I did. Perhaps we both did.

"Harder, baby. Fuck this pussy harder," she urged, her nails digging into the skin of my thighs, marking me as hers. I responded with a fierce growl, my movements becoming more urgent, desperate even, as I chased my own release. My orgasm recklessly surged through my body. It was fast and beautiful.

"Fuck," I cursed under my breath, the word tinged with wonder and something comparable to awe as I released my seed.

I'd never been inside anyone tighter or wetter than Zahra. She was lucky she was already mine. If she weren't, I'd kill every nigga who got in my way and move Hell and Earth to make it so.

"Yes. Just like that, baby. Don't stop. I'm yours," she confessed.

The rest of her words were lost as I collapsed onto her, our bodies spent from the intensity of our union. My arms enveloped her, my embrace a fortress in the aftershocks of our uninhibited passion. I could've spent a million hours buried deep inside her, and it still wouldn't have quenched my thirst.

"You can't ever leave me now," I said, my voice low and fierce as if I were speaking a vow.

I looked down to see her smiling against the warmth of my chest, feeling the steady thrum of my heartbeat. She brought her gaze to meet mine, and I saw the truth reflected at me.

"Where else would I go?" she whispered, sealing her question with a kiss that spoke of endless nights like this one, where the world would fall away and leave only us.

Zahra

ne week later.

Seven days had passed since XL's barbershop burned down and my run-in with Sienna at his cousin's wedding. Things had been quiet between us. We'd started sleeping in the same bed since we'd been intimate, but it didn't matter. He'd been working nonstop to find out who burned down his shop, and he hadn't stayed at the apartment much.

I sat in the living room, trying to think of something nice I could do for him. I struggled to think of a gift for someone who seemingly had it all. At least all I could give him. I was powerless to rebuild the one thing I knew he wanted most: his shop. My mind wandered as I thought about the little things that made him smile. He loved his freshly brewed coffee in the mornings, especially after he added his sweet almond milk creamer. He enjoyed cooking and was always itching to try a good recipe, particularly those he could add to his restaurant menu. And he had a soft spot for lo-fi hip-hop music, often playing it in the background while he cheffed it up in the kitchen.

As I considered those things, I realized how much my feelings for him had grown since we'd consummated our marriage of convenience. What started as a simple arrangement had snowballed into something much more profound. In his absence, I found myself missing him more and more with each passing day, wanting to be there for him just like he'd been there for me.

I'd never expected to feel the way I did for him, but seeing XL so stressed and determined to find out who'd set fire to his shop made me want to support him more. I decided to clean up around the apartment and put together a small care package for whenever he returned home. I put on a fresh pot of his favorite Colombian coffee blend, ordered a cookbook online with recipes I knew he'd want to try, and set up a lo-fi hip-hop playlist of tunes. It wasn't extravagant, but I hoped my act of kindness would speak to his love language by bringing him comfort and reminding him that he wasn't alone, despite how he may have felt.

I finally felt up to tackling the deep cleaning around the apartment I'd been putting off. My eyes scanned the living room—a few cups and a bowl on the coffee table hadn't made their way to the sink to be washed, and a striped Sherpa blanket haphazardly tossed over the couch.

With a determined sigh, I tied my long hair into a high bun, threw on my favorite 2000s R&B playlist, and pulled out cleaning supplies underneath the kitchen sink. Just as I knelt to spray the coffee table, there was a knock at the door. It was sharp and unexpected, echoing through the apartment and jarring me from my cleaning zone. My heart leaped into my throat, and before I could decide what to do next, I heard muffling on the other side of the door before it unlocked and opened.

"Shit," I hissed.

Panicked, I found my feet, raced down the hall, and ducked into the first bedroom. I peeked around the corner, and my breath caught in my chest. I recognized the two men who tramped inside—they were XL's cousins from the wedding. They looked around the apartment, clearly checking in on him, but he wasn't there. *Fuck. Fuck. Fuck. What am I going to do?*

"Where the fuck this nigga at? His phone is still going straight to voicemail," I heard one of them say.

They trekked down the hallway, still calling out his name. I tried to stay hidden, but they soon spotted me, their eyes narrowed in suspicion.

"Who the fuck are you?" the tall one with the brown skin asked.

Knocked off my square, I blurted out the first thing that came to mind, seeing as though I'd left out all the cleaning supplies. "I-I'm the cleaning lady."

By the doubtful looks on their faces, I knew they didn't buy my lie at first. They began drilling me with questions, their tone growing more insistent.

The other cousin, whose wedding I attended, stepped forward, looking me up and down. "Cleaning lady? You don't look like a fuckin' cleaning lady."

"Sorry, I'm out of uniform. I wasn't supposed to work today. Last minute schedule change."

"How long ago did he hire you?"

"A few months ago," I answered.

"And how much does he pay you?"

My mind raced, but I was determined to answer them and sound as convincing as possible. "I come twice a month. He pays my company three hundred and fifty dollars per session, depending on whether any extra services are added."

"You seen my cousin since you been here?"

"No."

"Then how'd you get in?"

"He leaves a key," I explained.

His cousins exchanged glances, still unconvinced but starting to back down. I knew I had to get out of there before they asked any more questions or started looking too hard around the space and noticed my things.

"I can come back later," I blurted out.

I slipped past them, my heart jerking against its tethers as I swiped my purse off the kitchen counter and hurried out of the apartment. As soon as I got outside to my car, I took a deep breath, trying to settle my bouncing nerves. The surprise encounter had shaken me, but I was relieved I managed to get away without revealing my true identity.

As I trekked down the street, my thoughts turned to Kendrick. I wondered why he hadn't answered his phone for his cousins and decided to give him a call. I pulled out my phone and tapped his name. The phone didn't even ring. It went straight to voicemail, like his cousins said. I sighed. I had to keep my head down and stay out of sight until I could contact him.

ABOUT HALF AN HOUR LATER, I PARKED OUTSIDE A COFFEE SHOP called Mocha Brews and decided to pick up some new coffee beans to add to XL's care package. When I stepped out of the car, I spotted Sienna walking inside. My heart skipped a beat, but being out in public surrounded by strangers gave me the confidence to speak to her more freely. The door chimed as I sailed through it. Sienna stood in line wearing a stretchy black jumpsuit, with her hair pulled up into a high bun. I cleared my throat, and she looked over her shoulder, recognizing me immediately. Her eyes were filled with curiosity and a hint of concern as she fully turned to face me.

"Zahra?"

"Hey, Sienna..." I looked down at her belly. She had to be at least five or six months pregnant. "I didn't get to tell you before, but congratulations on your pregnancy."

"Thanks. What brings you to Vegas? First the wedding, now my favorite coffee shop. It's not giving coincidence anymore."

"Yeah. I know. I didn't expect to see you here either."

"So, you live here now?"

"For the meantime, yeah."

"When'd you leave Miami?"

I hesitated for a moment, unsure of how much to reveal. But I decided to be somewhat transparent with her. "It's complicated."

She frowned, clearly unsatisfied with my vague answer, as she rested her hand on her belly. "I've got time."

I sighed. "Okay."

"You can start by telling me why you were at my brother-in-law's wedding a week ago."

My eyes widened in surprise before trickling down to the diamond secured around her ring finger. One of XL's cousins was Sienna's husband. What a small fuckin' world.

"I didn't know he was your brother-in-law."

She sighed as she shifted her weight from one foot to the other. Before she could say anything, the barista called for the next person in line, and it was her turn. I half expected her to leave once she received her herbal tea, but she stepped aside and waited for me. I walked over to her after I received the coffee beans for XL.

"You got time to sit?" she quizzed.

"Yeah."

"Then let's sit."

We found a vacant table in the back and took our seats. "Look, I know us running into each other was weird, but I promise you I'm not trying to start any trouble."

"Now I'm even more confused. What the hell is really going on, Zahra? Why did you say what you said about being... *dead*?" she asked, whispering her final word as if it were cursed.

I took a deep breath, deciding to give her a bit more context without revealing everything. "I'm here because I needed a fresh start. As for the wedding, I met a guy, and we decided to crash. That's it."

"Why'd you leave Miami?"

"Because things in Miami got… complicated."

She studied me momentarily, and her poker-faced expression was hard to read. I could tell she had more questions, but I wasn't sure how much more I could safely tell her without blowing up my life and XL's, too, especially with the knowledge that Sienna's husband was his cousin. He'd gone against his family to spare my life. I was sure they'd want to finish the job if they found out I was still alive.

Frustrated, Sienna pinched her lips together. "You say you're not here to start trouble, but it also sounds like there's a lot of shit you're leaving out. I want the full story, Zahra, and I want it now."

It had been over six years since we'd last seen each other, and despite the turn of events, I felt a mix of nostalgia being in her presence again.

"It's not something I can talk about right now. Please keep what you know to yourself. I need time to figure things out."

She sighed as she placed a hand on her belly, her expression softening as we traded glances. "You were seriously the last person I expected to see here in Vegas," she said, seemingly changing the subject.

I sighed. "Yeah, it's been a long time. A lot has changed since high school. You, me, and Zyon used to be thick as thieves once upon a time."

A ghost of a smile appeared on her face. "Yeah, we were. I remember when we snuck in and raided that old man's hotel room at that nice ass hotel in South Beach and almost got caught."

I chuckled, the memory bringing comfort from a time when everything seemed a lot simpler. "I thought we were going to jail that night."

"Me too. Zyon always had the best jobs when we were in high school."

"Or had the hook up to someone who did."

She nodded. "True."

"Speaking of your cousin, I ran into her a few weeks back," I mentioned.

Sienna's expression changed almost instantly, a hint of irritation flickering in her eyes at the mention of her cousin. "Oh."

"Did she tell you?"

"No. She and I don't speak anymore."

"Seriously? Why not?"

"Things got weird between us after my ex got out of prison. It was never the same between us after that."

I frowned. "Damn. Does she even know you're pregnant?"

Sienna shrugged, her unsureness clear. "I don't know what she knows, and I don't care. I've got too much other shit going on in my life right now to be worried about her and whatever shit she's got going on."

For some reason, I felt compelled to offer her a word of caution.

"I know that's your family and all, but just be careful. Zy was always a bit of a hater. I'm sure she wouldn't want to see us sitting here together after all these years."

Sienna sighed, her gaze firm and resolute. "I appreciate your concern, but I'm grown. I do what I want."

I nodded, respecting her independence as I watched her sip her tea.

"I never really understood what happened between you two. I know we were family, but y'all used to be inseparable," Sienna acknowledged.

Growing up, Zyon's natural-born mischievous streak always made her the life of the party and the most popular girl around our way. She had a way of making even the drab moments of life feel interesting. No wonder everyone she hung around, even me, found her bad-girl vibe infectious.

My expression hardened slightly as I glanced away, my thoughts reverting to the past. My brother hadn't been immune to her charm either.

"Zo happened. When she started dating my twin brother behind my back... or was it when she started cheating on him? I don't know. Everything got so tangled and messy once I found out and told her she needed to tell him or I would. That bitch didn't have the balls to break my brother's heart, so I had to do it. That's what drove the wedge between us."

Sienna's brows snapped together in confusion. "She told me he cheated on her."

I sucked my teeth. "That's bullshit, and she knows it. I caught her fucking Lil Terry that lived in the neighborhood across the tracks. She confessed it had been going on for a while, and that's when I gave her the ultimatum. And what did she do? Run off to Vegas with you and never looked back."

Sienna shook her head. "I'm sorry. I didn't know."

I nodded, a half-smile forming on my lips. "But life moves on, right? You live, and you learn who your friends and enemies are."

"That's true. How is Lorenzo anyway?"

I dipped my head, feeling a pang of sadness in my chest as my expression turned more serious. "He died some months back."

I could see the pain in her eyes as she covered her mouth in shock. "Oh my God. I'm so sorry."

She reached across the table and squeezed my hand, offering a small comforting gesture.

"Thank you."

Of our trio, Sienna had always been the calmer, more level-headed one. She wasn't the kind of girl who had her entire life planned out, but her demeanor and ability to let her creativity be her compass balanced out her cousin's wild, childish antics. Still, she wasn't immune to Zyon's temptress charm. Her cousin was the type to always be cooking up a new scheme or getting us into trouble, and we were too young, dumb, and broke not to go along with it.

As Sienna and I continued talking, I started to feel lightheaded. It hit me suddenly, a wave of dizziness mixed with nausea that made the room spin and my stomach churn. I quickly opened my purse and realized with a sinking feeling that I'd left my medication at the house and hadn't taken it for the day yet.

Fuck. I can't go back to the apartment. It's too risky. And I don't want to worry Sienna.

I tried to steady my thoughts by repeatedly telling myself I'd be okay. I took a deep breath and chiseled a strained smile into my features, trying to act normal.

"Excuse me. I need to use the bathroom. I'll be right back."

Sienna chuckled and went to stand up alongside me. "I've got to go too. This baby's happy place seems to be right on my bladder."

As soon as I stepped away from the table, another wave of dizziness crashed into me. My limbs became weightless as the room spun, and I felt my legs give out from under me before I could catch myself. The last thing I saw was the worried look on Sienna's face before everything went black.

XI

I stood at Big Mama's grave, gripping the bouquet and watching the light breeze rustle the delicate petals. It had been a week from hell since my barbershop burned to the ground. I went by there every day, staring at the remains and plotting my revenge. As the days passed, I sought guidance from Big Mama, the only person who always seemed to have the answers. She'd always been my rock. Even with her gone, I still felt her spirit with me.

I had my phone turned off since I'd woken up to help me disconnect from all the madness and hopefully find the clarity I was searching for. After spending some time at her gravesite, thinking and talking to her in my head, I decided it was time to head to the restaurant. I drew in a deep breath, feeling a little anxious as I went to turn my phone back on and tune back in to reality.

Almost instantly, my phone buzzed with back-to-back notifications. One message caught my eye—from one of the managers letting me know that my restaurant had been nominated for a local award, and a reporter from a popular online food and lifestyle publication wanted to interview me at noon for a feature in their Tastemakers section.

I glanced at the gold watch adorning my left wrist. I had an hour. Gentleness touched my lips as gratitude surged through me. It was as if Big Mama had given me the nudge I needed from beyond the grave, reminding me not to dwell on what I'd lost but to focus on what I had right in front of me—my loyal family, my successful soul food restaurant, and Zahra, the beautiful woman who my feelings had grown deeper for.

Thank you, Big Mama. I needed this. I needed to be reminded that there's still a lot to be grateful for.

I quickly replied to the message, agreeing to do the interview within the next hour. It was an opportunity I couldn't pass up, not just for the recognition but for the much needed morale boost that came with it. As I headed to the restaurant, I started to mentally prepare for the interview while reminding myself to stay focused on the positive shit I had going on.

I WAS AT THE RESTAURANT, SITTING ACROSS FROM THE YOUNG female reporter who'd come to interview me for the online publication. The familiar sound of clinking dishes and conversations among the customers eating lunch filled the air.

"Thanks for meeting with me today. I came here during the week of your grand opening, and everything I had was amazing. Your menu is very flavor-forward. Can you explain how your background influenced your cooking?"

"Well, first, thank you for coming. I'm glad you enjoyed your meal with us. As far as my background, food has always been a staple in my family, especially for my grandmother, Big Mama. I grew up with food at damn near every single family gathering, whether it was birthdays, weddings, or funerals. Food and fellowship, that's the best way to do it."

"You were close with her?"

"Extremely close. My cousins and I grew up in my Big Mama's

house, so I learned to cook very early. The first thing she would say to us when we walked through the door from school or wherever was, 'Are you hungry?' or 'Did you eat?' She always made sure we left the house with full bellies."

"That's love right there. So, your cousins also know how to cook?" the reporter probed.

"Nah. Not like me. Cooking was me and Big Mama's thing. She passed away last year, so I'm still in a little bit of a transition period now. But in the past year, I feel like I've probably gotten even closer with her just by cooking her signature meals and putting the same amount of love into them as she did."

A smile breezed over the reporter's mouth. "Wow. That's inspiring. Besides cooking, is there anything else you enjoy most about being in the kitchen?"

"Besides cooking, one of my favorite things is plating the meal. Aside from the flavorful food, I want to keep you engaged with what's on the plate; the aesthetic of it all, you know? Just like an artist, I've got a creative eye for that. I want all your senses tingling when the plate gets delivered to your table," I answered.

Despite my stress, the interview had been going well. It felt good to talk about the success of my restaurant, especially since our doors hadn't been open for long. She continued to ask me intriguing questions like the kitchen item I couldn't live without, how it felt to be nominated for a Vegas Foodie Award, and what music I listened to in the kitchen.

"Do you think food is a love language? If so, why?"

I scrunched my shoulders against my neck, considering my answer before I parted my lips. "I don't see why not. Food is nourishment, and it's a way for us to feed not only our bodies and the bodies of the people we love, but our souls too."

She nodded while parting her lips, preparing to ask her next question when my phone buzzed in my pocket. I pulled it out to silence the vibrations and glanced at the screen. It was a call from an unknown number. Usually, I would've ignored it, but something in my spirit urged me to answer.

"I'm sorry. Can you excuse me for a second? I need to take this."

I pushed myself away from the table and stepped away as I answered the phone. "Who dis?"

The voice on the other end was urgent and filled with concern. "Hello. Is this Mr. Patton? My name is Naomi Stevens, and I'm a nurse at Sunrise Valley Hospital. Your wife was rushed here via ambulance after passing out in a coffee shop," she explained.

My heart skipped a beat as sweat glazed my forehead. "Oh my God. Is she okay?" I inquired, propelling myself up.

"I can't give out any medical information over the phone, but she's stable, and the doctors are running tests."

I felt a lump in my throat as I tried to silence my emotions to process all the information. "Thank you. I'm on my way right now. I'll be there as soon as I can."

"You're welcome. I'll notify the woman who rode in the ambulance with her."

"A woman? What woman?"

"I didn't get her name, but she's pregnant and looked really shaken up. She's still in the emergency room waiting area."

"I'm on my way," I reiterated.

I hung up the phone, my mind spinning with worry for Zahra. I wondered who the pregnant woman was and how the hospital knew to call me in the first place, but I remembered I was the only number saved in Zahra's phone. I turned on my heels to walk back toward the reporter, who looked concerned by my sudden change in demeanor.

"Is everything all right?" she inquired.

I shook my head, trying to keep my voice from breaking. "I'm sorry, but I have to go. My wife is in the hospital. Can we reschedule the rest of the interview?"

The reporter nodded quickly with understanding in her eyes. "Of course. Take care of what you need to. I hope your wife is okay."

I didn't even wait to tell her goodbye. I raced out of the restaurant, my thoughts consumed with getting to Zahra's side. I couldn't lose her, not now. Not before I told her how I felt about her. As I sped to the hospital, I shot a prayer up to God that she'd be okay and that I'd get there in time. When we initially agreed to get married, we did it with plans of getting a divorce once her health situation was under control. But the longer we stayed husband and wife, the more I started to want to stick by our vows—for richer or for poorer, in sickness and in health. All that shit. I wanted her forever.

I broke into a jog, racing toward the hospital entrance and thundering toward the information desk as I tried to recover my breath.

"I'm here for Zahra Patton. A nurse called and told me she was brought in earlier after passing out in a coffee shop."

"Are you family, sir?" the nurse asked.

"I'm her husband," I confirmed.

The nurse directed me to the emergency room, and my feet took flight down the hall, racing to get to the woman I'd given my heart to without even noticing. I shot on unsteady legs to the nurse's station, demanding to see Zahra. I was met with the news that she'd been taken back for testing and was directed to wait in the emergency waiting area until a doctor came out to provide an update.

I sat in the waiting area, feeling helpless. My right leg bounced with anxiety as I waited for any news on Zahra. Worry gnawed at my gut. Suddenly, the sliding emergency room doors parted, and my cousins, Ahsan and Amir, rushed in, their expressions confused and concerned. Only, they weren't looking for me. I'd been so focused on getting to Zahra that I hadn't reached out to return any of their calls or texts. I kept my eyes stationed on them as they raced over to Sienna, who stood to greet them in the opposite corner. *Was she the pregnant woman who had come in the ambulance with Zahra, or were they there because something was going on with her?*

I shot to my feet, and before I could announce myself, Ahsan pinned me with a direct lens. His eyes doubled in size as he turned to face me.

"XL? Nigga, where the hell have you been? We've been chasing you down all day. We went by the restaurant, and someone said you rushed to the hospital to check on your *wife*. I told them they had to be confused because you're not married. But we show up, and here you are. What the hell is going on?" Ahsan probed.

Amir looked just as puzzled as his brother, his eyes narrowing as he looked at me, then back at Sienna. "We were out running around trying to find your ass when Sienna called Ahsan and asked him if he could pick her up from the hospital. He asked why, and she said she rode in the ambulance with somebody who fainted at a coffee shop. Now we get here and see you. What the fuck is up, XL?"

I drew a lungful of air. It was past time for me to break my silence and come clean about sparing Zahra's life and marrying her too. I couldn't keep it from them any longer. I didn't want to, especially when there was a chance I might lose her.

"Listen, I need to tell y'all something I should've told you months ago. They weren't lying at the restaurant. I did say that. I do have a wife," I declared.

The three of them stared at me, eyes broadcasting surprise. None of them could've predicted my announcement.

"Zahra's *your* wife?" Sienna probed. "Like, you two are actually married to each other? Like hand on the bible? Paperwork signed?"

I confirmed her questions with a simple nod. "How do you two even know each other?"

Before she could answer, Ahsan butted in with a question of his own. "Who the fuck is Zahra, and when did she become your wife? You've never mentioned anything about dating, let alone getting married."

I dipped my chin in a nod, feeling my secret's weight finally lifted off my shoulders. "I know. It was quick and unexpected."

"Quick is an understatement. Who the fuck is she?" Amir probed.

My head tilted toward the sliding emergency room doors. I'd tell them the whole truth, but it wasn't for everyone within earshot to hear. I led our group outside and stepped off to ensure our privacy before speaking.

"You remember the night we handled Rico, and I brought y'all outside? Zahra is the girl from the trunk," I confessed.

I locked eyes with Amir first, knowing I'd gone against what he'd asked me to do. He grunted. "I thought you said you'd handle it."

"I know what I said, but there's more to it."

"How much more?" Ahsan interjected.

"She's sick... She's got a rare, life-threatening blood disorder. The treatments were expensive, and she didn't have the money or insurance to cover them."

"Is that why you married her? To add her to your health insurance?" Sienna quizzed, hitting the nail right on the head.

"Yeah. It was a crazy arrangement, and we kept it private. It wasn't supposed to get out, at least not like this."

Ahsan's stern expression softened as he processed my words. He traded glances with his brother. "You think she was the one from earlier?"

"The housekeeper?" Amir asked.

"She wasn't no fuckin' housekeeper, nigga. It all makes sense now, the way she ran outta there so fast. It had to be her."

"I ran into her at the coffee shop I like to go to," Sienna added. "We talked for a while and got up to use the bathroom when she fainted. It freaked me the hell out, so I called nine-one-one and rode with her here. They were asking me questions about her emergency contacts and allergies and I didn't know any answers, so I gave her phone to one of the nurses."

"Baby, how the hell do you know her?" Ahsan asked his wife.

"She's from Miami. She used to be Zyon's best friend. The three of us hung out a lot, so we were cool. We haven't seen each other in years, though. Then, all of a sudden, I ran into her in the bathroom at Amir's reception. She immediately started acting all weird and told me she was supposed to be dead."

"That's because she is," Amir blurted out. "But XL chose to lie to us instead, knowing you found her with our fuckin' opp, nigga!"

"I know where I found her, but it wasn't what I thought. She was there to kill Rico for setting up her brother."

"She did tell me he died," Sienna joined in.

"How do you know she's telling the truth? How do you know she's not tied to whoever burned down your shop?" Amir questioned.

"The thought crossed my mind, but it wasn't her. She wasn't lying about her brother. I looked into it. It checked out. His death was ruled an unsolved homicide by Miami PD."

Amir grunted. "I still don't trust it or her. And I don't think you should either. For all we know, the bitch could be playing the long game and setting us all up from the inside! You know bitches in Miami love to scam."

"Chill," Sienna snapped, slicing her gaze through Amir.

My brow furrowed. "Did I give you this much shit when you decided to impregnate the sister of one of our opps, nigga? No. I told you I'd be fuckin' there for you because we were family. I told you I'd ride with you because I knew you were capable of making your own goddamn decisions. You made yours then, and I'm making mine now. Nobody fuckin' touches Zahra because I'm in love with her," I affirmed.

Ahsan's eyes tore wide. "You're in love with her?" he repeated with a questioning tone.

I nodded, my voice steady despite the chaotic emotions that had my heart gunning into overdrive. "Yeah, I am. And I need to be here for her, just like she's been there for me."

Amir shook his head, seemingly still trying to wrap his mind around everything. "Look, I'm all for happy endings and shit, but this is a lot to take in, nigga. You gon' have to give me a minute."

"Take all the time you need, nigga. You ain't gotta understand it. You just gotta respect it."

After a few seconds of silence, Ahsan stepped forward. "You're right. Whatever you need, we're here for you like always."

I nodded. Even in their skepticism, I was grateful for their backing. We dapped each other up one at a time. "Thanks. Right now, all I'm focused on is Zahra. She's been through a lot, and I'm not ready to let her go. God already snatched Big Mama from me. I won't let him have Zahra too. I refuse."

"Then get back in there, nigga. Go get your girl," Amir encouraged, shooing me back toward the door.

As I waited anxiously in the hospital, a middle-aged female doctor with brown hair and gray roots finally emerged. My heart pounded in my chest as I prepared myself for the update.

"Are you here for Zahra Patton?"

My eyes flashed wide open. "Yes. I'm her husband."

"I'm Doctor Ritter. We got your wife's test results back, and I'm afraid the plasma treatments and corticosteroids aren't working as well as we thought they were. Your wife will need surgery to remove her spleen immediately."

My mind raced with worry, but I knew what to do. Zahra had no choice but to live because there was no me without her. Without hesitation, I stepped forward. "Do whatever you have to do to save her life. I don't care how long it takes, and I don't care about the cost. You go back there and don't come out of that fuckin' operating room until you've saved my wife."

Doctor Ritter nodded. "We'll do everything we can. I'll keep you updated after surgery."

As the doctor turned to leave, a wave of emotions washed over me. At that moment, I realized just how much I loved Zahra. I knew I needed to tell her how I felt. The thought of losing her was unbearable. And now that my family knew the truth about us, the last thing I wanted to do was get a divorce.

Zahra

I stirred awake, my eyes slowly fluttering open and adjusting to the harsh glare of the hospital lights surrounding me. As my vision became more precise, I started to look around. The walls were coated a muted yellow and were decorated with a few generic yet serene paintings of the beach. The same oil paintings were in my old room during my last hospital stay. A heart monitor beeped quietly to my left, showcasing my vital signs. I should've been happier than I was to be still alive, but I was too drugged up on medication to think straight.

Across the room, the partially drawn curtains draped over the window allowed a sliver of outside light to filter in. As I shifted my gaze to the right, I noticed XL sitting by my bedside, his tired, brown eyes filled with concern as he stared back at me. His presence was a soothing reminder that I wasn't alone despite the cold, clinical hospital room.

"Hey, you," I said, voice scratchy.

"Hey. How are you feeling?" he asked softly, his voice trembling slightly. "The doctor said your spleen surgery went well, just waiting on your latest lab results to come in."

My hand instinctively went to my abdomen, feeling the dull ache where my spleen used to be. I couldn't believe I had to have the surgery after all.

"I'm still here. That's half the battle right there, right?"

"Right. You're gonna beat this, Zahra. Now that you've had the surgery, you'll be okay."

I smiled weakly, touched by his ability to build castles in the air but cautious of giving him false hope. "Thanks."

"Do you need anything? Want me to get you something to drink? Ice chips? Fluff your pillow?"

A sly smirk crept up one side of my mouth. "Are you in danger of becoming a gentleman, Kendrick Patton?"

"I'm being serious. I wanna make sure you're good and have everything you need. I never should've let you out of my sight in the first place," he said, voice riddled with unwarranted guilt as he placed a cup of water on the tray table before me. "I've been so consumed with this barbershop shit that I wasn't able to see anything else."

"What happened to me wasn't your fault."

"Why'd you leave the house in the first place?" he inquired, refusing to acknowledge the truth.

"Because your cousins showed up looking for you. I had to think of something quick, so I lied and told them I was the damn cleaning lady. I left in a hurry and forgot to take my meds."

He frowned. "Damn, yo. I'm so sorry I wasn't fuckin' there."

"I was at the coffee shop, trying to do something nice for you. I wanted to get you your favorite coffee beans. I was talking to Sienna when I got dizzy and blacked out. That's the last thing I remember."

"How do you know Sienna anyway?" he probed.

I sighed before finally wrapping my lips around the straw and sending cold liquid down my dehydrated throat. "We have history from back in Miami. Her cousin, Zyon, and I used to be close, but not anymore. Now that bitch hates me as much as I hate her, but that's a story for a different day. I should've told you about it sooner, but I didn't want to freak you out after I saw her at the wedding."

His thick brows twitched toward each other. "What's the issue with her cousin?"

I eyed the IV in my arm. "I don't wanna talk about that ho right now. She makes my ass itch."

He chuckled softly. "This world is small as hell."

"And getting smaller every day."

"I'm just glad you're going to be okay."

"I appreciate you looking on the bright side for me, but I don't want you hoping against hope," I explained before taking another sip of water.

He took my hand in his, and I felt a lump forming in my throat. "My Big Mama always used to say where there's life, there's hope. Thinking I'd lost you only made me realize I'm in love with you, Zahra," he admitted, his serious gaze locking onto mine. "I know us getting married was just a means to an end, a way to get you the health insurance you needed, but I don't want this to end. I want to stay married."

His sweet words tugged at my heartstrings, and I felt a flame of sadness in my chest, winding it tighter than yarn on a spool. The lump in my throat made it impossible to speak, and my eyes stung, welling up with an intense pressure behind them that I tried like hell to hold back. My body shook with tattered breath as I tried to keep a lid on my emotions and remember why we did what we did in the first place. We had an arrangement, and I couldn't get emotionally attached. No more than I already had, that is. I was already in too deep, any further, and I'd risk drowning in him.

I inhaled a stuttery breath, trying to keep my voice steady despite the emotions churning inside me. "But I don't," I confessed.

His handsome face fell at the sound of my words, and I knew they'd pierced his heart like a Hulk punch to the gut. "What? Why not?"

"You don't want to be tethered to someone with health issues for the rest of your life. I won't put you through that."

A spark of defiance ignited in his eyes as he swung his head in a no. "You think you're protecting me, but all you're doing is pushing me away because you're scared," he said, his voice barely hiding the pain we both knew he was in. "After all this time, do you really believe I wouldn't want to stay by your side, no matter what?"

I looked away as more tears stirred behind my eyes and weakly squeezed his hand. "I can't let you tether your heart to mine. It's not fair to you."

"Who are you to decide what's fair when it comes to how I feel about you? You need me to repeat it? Because I will. I fuckin' love you, Zahra, and I don't plan on losing you. I chose you. In sickness and in health, remember?"

I felt the wall I'd built crumbling with every new brick laid, but I forced myself to stay rooted in my decision. "I just... I can't put you through that. It's my choice."

"Let me decide what I can fuckin' handle. I wanna be here for you, for better or worse. Isn't that what we agreed on?" he pleaded, pain seeping from his chocolate orbs.

My heart bled at his words. He was right, but I couldn't shake the fear of becoming a permanent burden to him. He had so much going for him, and his steps had already been ordered. I didn't want to slow him down. "I need time to think," I said, refusing to make eye contact with him.

He nodded, understanding but refusing to give up. "Take all the time you need, but know I'm not going anywhere. You're my wife, and I'm right here, Zahra, and I always will be. I put that on everything I love."

The room fell into a heavy, intense silence, both of us lost in the sea of our thoughts as the burden of our disagreement hung between us. Finally, he stood to his feet and walked out. The sight of his broad shoulders slumping as he reached the door hit me with a wave of conflicting emotions. It was an overwhelming ache in my chest mixed with loss and sadness. It felt something like grief but not quite. He was right. I did push away someone who genuinely cared about me. But I'd done it to save him, even if he couldn't see it.

The door closed behind him, and suddenly, the room seemed colder and more sterile. Loneliness settled into my bones, a feeling I hadn't felt since my brother died. My mind replayed our conversation and his heartfelt plea for us to stay together. He'd told me he loved me, and I couldn't bring myself to say it back, no matter how badly I wanted to.

I was torn between my desire to protect him from the future pain of losing me and the heartache of knowing I'd condemned myself to a life of solitude by pushing away the love and support of the last nigga on Earth who wanted to be by my side. My decision to break up with XL was because I wanted to protect him from the burden of my health issues, but the emotional toll on my heart had proven to be more than I could afford.

XI

I left Zahra's hospital room, feeling a massive weight settle onto my chest. Being rejected by the woman I loved cut me deeper than any knife. The pain and frustration intensified with each step I took away from her side. My mind was a tangled ball of emotions—anger, sadness, confusion, and helplessness all rolled into one.

I'd hoped that my love and commitment would be enough to convince Zahra to want to stay married, but her decision to push me away for my own good had me feeling a different kind of heartbreak. I knew she was only acting out of fear, but it didn't make her refusal to stay married any easier to take on the chin.

Once I stepped outside the hospital, I paused near the emergency room entrance, leaning against a cold metal railing to settle my racing thoughts before I got behind the wheel. The dry Vegas air offered little clarity. Zahra's words, stuck on repeat in my mind, burned hotter than the heat—she didn't want to stay married to me. The ground underneath my feet felt like it was seconds from slipping away. I felt like a fool for allowing myself to marry her. To catch feelings for her. To give my heart to her. To pray over her. *Fuck.*

The loud sirens from an approaching ambulance snapped me back into reality. My eyes darted toward it as it screeched to a halt in front of the emergency room entrance. The broken organ in the center of my chest managed to skip a beat when I saw Brandi, Amir's ex, stepping out before the paramedics brought out her boyfriend on a stretcher. He looked in pain, and I couldn't help but overhear the frantic explanations she gave to a cop—something about a drive-by shooting at a red light on their way home from dinner. The scene unfolding in front of my eyes only fueled my curiosity. Who the hell had been bold enough to run down on her man in public, and why?

My need for answers gnawed at me, overpowering my better judgment and the will to get in the car and drive home. Unable to resist the urge to question her about the fire at my barbershop, I went back inside. By the time I reached Brandi, the doctors had already wheeled her boyfriend into emergency surgery.

"Yo, Brandi." My voice boomed as I called out to her louder than anticipated.

She snapped her neck in my direction with an irritated look. "XL? What the fuck are you doing here?"

"What happened?"

Brandi folded her arms across her chest while shooting me a knifing look. "How do I know you didn't have anything to do with the fucking shooting and aren't just here to make sure he's dead?" she popped off, her fear and frustration evident in her wild ass accusation.

"Where'd he get shot?"

"You switched sides and workin' for the cops now? Because if not, I don't owe you an explanation."

"C'mon, Brandi."

"If you didn't have shit to do with it, then why do you care?" she snapped, tone like hot coals.

I stiffened my gaze at her. "You know what, fuck it. I need to ask you something else. Where were you on the seventeenth, the night my barbershop burned down?" I asked, my question spilling out before I could second-guess myself about why I approached her.

"How the fuck was I supposed to know your barbershop burned down, nigga? I'm not plugged in with your family anymore!"

"I know you fuckin' knew. By now, everybody knows. Now answer the goddamn question. Where the fuck were you?"

Brandi sucked her teeth, her teary eyes spewing hate as she glanced down at her nigga's blood stains all over the front of her designer outfit. "Seriously? You're asking me that now?" she queried, her tone sharp and annoyed. "I had nothing to do with that goddamn fire!"

I grilled her. "I'm not fuckin' convinced."

"Not that it's any of your business, but I was out of town with my man."

"Prove it then."

The only follow-up I'd gotten from the police since the fire was that they believed the person who set my shop on fire was a male. Footage from one of the traffic cameras revealed a blurry image of a male walking with something in his hand near the shop the night of the fire, but he had on a hood that shielded his face, and they couldn't I.D. the mothafucka. They also couldn't recover anything in their system from the partial prints left on the gas can.

Brandi smacked her cotton candy pink lips, giving me the stink-eye as if she had better shit to do. She aggressively scrolled through the phone she had clutched in her right hand.

"Look," she demanded, shoving the phone in my face. "Here's a video on my page of us from that night, geotagged in fuckin' San Diego, nigga. See? I told you we weren't even in Vegas!"

I raised a suspicious brow. "You expect me to believe that shit?"

Her orbs burned fury hot in frustration. "Believe whatever the fuck you want, XL. I don't care. I hate Amir for playing in my face the way he did. But, I heard his girl's little raggedy-ass hair business ain't doing so well, so maybe that's that nigga's karma. Nevertheless, maybe you niggas should focus on that instead of playing in my goddamn face, okay? I may have left a janky one-star review or two, but I didn't mess with your family. I'm smart enough to know better, and the last thing I give a fuck about is your goddamn barbershop. Do I look like I'm getting a fade any time soon, nigga? Exactly."

Still doubtful, I levied a glare at her as I sighed and leaned against a nearby wall. No matter how badly I wanted to name her and her man the culprits of the fire, the video evidence she'd shown me was undeniable. It couldn't have been Cannon on the traffic camera. "I don't know what the fuck to think anymore."

"Well, that's your problem. As you can see, I've got bigger fucking issues right now. I swear to God, if this nigga dies, I'm done with drug dealers. Done! Now move around, mothafucka!"

Her words hung in the air as she coldly brushed past me toward the waiting room, leaving me standing in the sterile corridor with more questions than answers swirling around in my head. Our encounter did nothing to unjumble the mess in my fractured heart. If anything, that shit added another complicated layer of confusion and uncertainty. With a heavy sigh, I turned and headed toward the exit, not entirely sure where to go next, both mentally and emotionally.

———

ONE WEEK LATER.

A WEEK LATER, I WAS BACK INSIDE MY RESTAURANT, SITTING AT the same table I'd initially met with the reporter. I felt colder and more reserved than before, but perhaps that was just my melancholy perspective casting a shadow over everything like a dark cloud. Since leaving the hospital with no woman and no leads, I'd vowed to throw myself into my restaurant, spending all day and night cooking and creating new recipes.

I knew Zahra had been released from the hospital, so I steered clear of the apartment altogether, coming in only when I was sure she was sound asleep to grab clothes or shit I needed from the kitchen. After weeks of waiting for more updates from the police, my frustration ate away at me from the inside out. The barbershop fire left a massive void in my life and the community. I couldn't afford to wait any longer for the police to do their fucking jobs.

I pushed those thoughts aside when the reporter arrived, her familiar bubbly demeanor slightly chilled as she sensed the shift in my attitude. She politely inquired about my mood, calling out the overtiredness in my eyes and the tension in my stiffened posture.

"I'm good, thanks. Let's knock this out," I responded briefly, my voice devoid of the enthusiasm I initially carried when we first met.

Throughout the interview, my responses remained clipped, damn near bordering on rude. The grace and genuine openness I'd shown her in our first interview had been replaced with an unemotional, almost machine-like objective to speed through her questions as quickly as possible.

Sensing my disinterest, she paused, hovering her purple pen over her open notepad and stopping the recording on her phone between us. "I mean no disrespect when I say this, Mr. Patton, but you seem very different from our last interview. You were kind and humble then, and today it's giving tell me you don't wanna be here without telling me you don't wanna be here. Are you sure everything is okay? Is your wife all right?"

I cut my gaze at her before softening it. I found a half smile for her, though it didn't quite reach my eyes, proving it looked as strained as it felt. "Just a lot on my mind. Please, let's keep going. I promise you I'm good. And for the record, I'm not here to discuss my personal life, only my restaurant."

She dipped her chin while pasting on a mouth-only smile of her own and pressing the start button on the recording again. The interview continued, and I repeatedly glanced at the expensive gold watch on my wrist, willing the minutes to go by faster. My feelings were turning me every way but loose, making it hard for me to focus. I couldn't stop my thoughts from drifting back to Zahra and our last conversation in her hospital room to the feeling of helplessness that I wore on my chest like a scarlet letter ever since.

Finally, we wrapped up. I stood and extended a handshake to the reporter. "Thank you for your time."

She nodded, her curiosity evident in her gaze, but she remained silent, respecting my need for privacy. "Sure thing. Take care of yourself."

As she turned to leave, I felt a surge of frustration bubbling up inside the pit of my stomach, like a squealing kettle about to boil over. The urge to break something, kill anything, was almost too much to bear. With no immediate outlet for my rage, I felt like I was closer and closer to losing my grip on my sanity and going batshit crazy.

Seeking solace, I called up Amir, hoping he'd provide a much needed distraction or at least some understanding. As soon as he picked up, he heard the distress in my voice. I couldn't hide it anymore. A nigga was down bad. We agreed to meet at the cigar bar, where the smoke and fellowship would drown out my heavy thoughts.

Amir looked up, his eyebrows raised in concern as he dapped me up. "Wassup, fam? You good?"

I shrugged as I drew in a deep breath, nostrils filling with the heavy aroma of tobacco in the air. "Been better."

He took a slow drag from his cigar. "How's your girl doing?"

I exhaled heavily, my anger apparent in how my broad shoulders tensed. "I don't want to talk about that."

He scoffed, calling my bluff. "Bullshit. Why not?"

"It's fuckin' complicated."

Amir shook his head, a smirk playing on his lips. "I still can't believe you got a whole wife, man. You? The forever bachelor?"

My lungs filled with smoke as I grumbled, the words escaping before I had the chance to filter them. "Didn't I just tell your bigheaded ass I didn't want to talk about it? Besides, it wasn't supposed to be like this. I wish I never did the shit in the first place."

Seeing the chaos behind my eyes, Amir leaned in, his voice

steady and sincere. "Says the nigga who doesn't wanna talk about it." I cut him an icy glare, and he surrendered his palms. "I'm just fuckin' with you. On the real, though, if the roles were reversed, and it was me sitting over there with the same sad mug you got on your face right now, I know you'd tell me to remember why I fell in love in the first place. We both know life can be messy as hell and shit hardly ever goes as planned. But running away or wishing things were different won't solve your problems. You gotta face that shit head-on. Soften that icy ass heart of yours, nigga. Your girl needs you. By the looks of it, you need her, whether you wanna admit it or not."

Amir's advice hit home for me in a way I didn't expect, each word chipping away at the iceberg I'd built around my heart after Zahra's rejection. I knew my cousin's counsel was sound, but bitterness and rage were still attached to me like a second skin.

Nodding, I muttered, "I hear you," though I refused to commit to letting go of my anger. The war raging between my heart and my ego was far from over.

"I still can't believe she and Sienna knew each other," Amir recalled, slicing through my trance. "She never mentioned it?"

"Nah. Not until the hospital. She said she used to be close to her cousin Zyon, but they had a falling out."

Amir paused as he raised a questioning brow. "Zyon? Why do I know that name for some reason?"

"I don't know," I answered with a lazy shrug while puffing my cigar.

"Nah, for real. I know that name for a reason," he said, pulling out his phone. I watched him tap at the screen and put the phone to his ear while nursing his glass of aged whiskey. "Hey, baby. Yeah, I'm still with XL. You and Eli good? You sure? All right. Hey, I got a quick question for you. Didn't you tell me a story about somebody named Zyon a while back? Oh shit. Yeah, that's right. I remember now. Thank you, baby. I love you. I'll see you in a little bit."

Amir ended the call, and I rolled my eyes. "You niggas are sickening with all that lovey-dovey shit."

He chuckled. "You sound like a hater."

"What did she say though?"

His expression hardened. "Ahsan should be here."

"What do you mean?"

"Let's go to the car."

"Why?" I probed.

"Because I think our problems might be bigger than we think."

I frowned as I stood to my feet. "Call him."

Amir nodded before calling his brother and putting it on speaker. He answered on the third ring. "Hello?"

"Yo, you got a minute?" Amir asked.

"Yeah, wassup?"

"You alone?"

"Yeah. Why?"

"We need to talk, and it's about Sienna's cousin Zyon," he informed us as we got into the car and started the engine. "And you're not going to like it."

"What's up?" Ahsan inquired, voice booming through Amir's car speakers.

As he set the phone in his center console, Amir's chest deflated with a heavy sigh. "It was the day of Rizzy's brother's funeral. We were about to leave the cemetery when she told me she'd meet me in the car. She walked over to a woman I'd never seen before. They had some words, and then she went on her way. We got in the car and did the same. I asked her what that was about and if she needed me to take care of anything for her. At the time, she told me no. Whatever it was, she'd handled it, so I left it at that. Then about a couple of months after she had Eli, she was still going through her postpartum and shit. She was down and really emotional. She'd cry a lot. One night, she talked to me about her brother, and the funeral day came up. That's when she first told me about the woman from the cemetery. It was Zyon, Sienna's cousin, and she told Nerissa that she and that snake Demario had some sort of an arrangement," Amir revealed.

"What kind of arrangement?" Ahsan interjected.

"I don't know the details. All I know is it was about money."

"Is that what Nerissa told you or what Zyon actually said to her?" I quizzed.

Amir huffed. "It's what Zyon told her, but that's not all Nerissa told me."

"What the fuck else is there?" Ahsan asked. I heard the panic in his rushed tone.

"She said that Zyon and Demario staged that robbery at Sienna's apartment. She heard them talking about it once over the phone when she stayed with him. She said she threatened Zyon to stay the fuck away or she'd tell Sienna the truth."

"That her cousin is a fucking liar and needs to be dealt with," Ahsan affirmed with a specific tone in his voice. "I knew that bitch was bad news the moment I met her. Sienna was just too blind to see it."

I knew that tone of his all too well. He wanted blood, and so did I. I sighed. Since we were all revealing information, I decided to inform them about my run-in with Brandi.

"I saw Brandi at the hospital last week," I announced.

Amir snapped his gaze in my direction. "What?"

"Her nigga got shot in a drive-by. I don't know if he made it."

"Fuck 'em," Amir grumbled. "We got bigger shit to deal with."

"She accused us of having something to do with that shit. I told her she was delusional."

Amir scoffed. "That pussy ass nigga ain't even worth the bullet."

"I questioned her about the barbershop," I continued. "They were in San Diego the night of the fire. She showed me proof."

"Doesn't mean she or that nigga couldn't have hired somebody to do their fuckin' dirty work," Amir alleged.

"She said she was smart enough to know not to fuck with us. And even though I don't like that bitch, I believe her."

Amir swung his head in contempt. "Nah. Y'all niggas don't know Brandi like I do. She's a petty ass bitch."

"So, you still think it was her?" Ahsan questioned, inserting himself back into the conversation.

"I'm just saying we'd be stupid to weed her out."

"Any other leads? Have you heard from the police?"

I sucked my teeth. "Nah. It's been weeks since the last update, and still no fuckin' answers. I'm tired of waiting for the police to do their goddamn jobs."

Amir nodded, understanding the urgency and the anger festering beneath my skin, just waiting to be unleashed. "I feel you. Tell me what you wanna do."

"Use that blurry ass picture we got from the police and put the word out on the street," I instructed, my voice firm. "I want every bit of information on the barbershop fire. Leave nothing or no one off the table. I'm ready to kill a nigga, and I want to do it by the end of this week," I growled.

We had connections and knew how to navigate the underbelly of the city. We'd find out from the streets if there were something to find out.

Amir nodded in agreement. "Say less. Consider it done."

"And what about this Zyon situation?" Ahsan added. "I'm not going to say shit to Sienna because she's pregnant, and I don't want to stress her out. But that doesn't mean I'm letting this bitch slide. She stole from my woman, which means she stole from me. She's got to be dealt with."

"Don't worry, we'll handle her too," Amir confirmed.

I felt a sense of steely satisfaction, knowing that steps were finally being taken to reveal the truth behind who was involved in the fire. My icy heart remained heavy with the weight of Zahra's decision and the loss of my shop. Taking things into my own hands gave me a sense of control. I clung to that power, knowing it was almost game time and the streets were about to go crazy.

Zahra

I wasn't feeling well. I was lying in bed with a fever and chills that sapped all my strength when I felt a sharp pain in my abdomen. I got up to go to the bathroom and looked in the mirror at my incision. It looked swollen with puss, and a deep sense of anxiety washed over me. It was mid-afternoon, but I called my doctor, and she told me to go to the hospital and get it checked out immediately.

At the hospital, the medical staff examined me and confirmed my worst fears—my incision was showing signs of infection. They gave me antibiotics and decided to keep me overnight for observation and tests to see how my body responded to the medication. The next thing I knew, I was gowned up and placed in a private room with an IV sticking out of my right arm.

As the hours ticked by and evening turned into night, I couldn't stop my thoughts from bouncing back and forth between my health and XL. The regret and sadness inside me released a chill over my bones whenever I allowed myself to dwell in my heartache. My decision to divorce XL gnawed at me. He'd given me time to think, and that I had, to the point where my brain hurt almost as much as my heart.

I wanted to call him, to hear his soothing, baritone voice tell me that everything would be okay, but the fear of his rejection kept me from pressing his name. Instead, I replayed the day I made the worst mistake of my life—breaking the heart of the man I loved. It earned its spot at the top of the list of things I wished to take back.

I WOKE UP A QUARTER PAST MIDNIGHT. MY HOSPITAL ROOM WAS silent and almost entirely dark, aside from the sliver of hallway light underneath the door. The loneliness quickly became overwhelming, and the familiar, ghostly chill appeared, popping goosebumps all over my skin.

I closed my eyes, and there he was: Kendrick, the man I'd grown to love and the secret yet sacred life we had shared over the past few months. Tears brimmed in the corners of my eyes as flashbacks of our time together flooded my mind. The ache to hear his voice was overwhelming, and I succumbed to my feelings that were deep enough to swim in.

My chest rattled with a lung-filling inhale as my heart jackhammered in my chest. It was time to set my pride aside. With trembling hands, I picked up my phone and pressed his name, mentally preparing myself for whatever might happen. Regardless, he deserved to know the truth—that I loved him even though it was the scariest fucking thing in the world for me to admit.

It rang once. Twice. Then, it went straight to voicemail.

My heart clunked to the pit of my stomach. He didn't answer. *Did he ignore my call?* Still, I didn't hang up. I listened for the beep signaling me to leave a message.

Beep.

I pressed through my heavy-heartedness and began to speak, my voice quivering with emotion. "H-hey... it's me. I know it's been a little while since we talked, and I'm sorry for calling so late. It's just… I'm in the hospital, and I've been thinking because that's all people do when they're lonely. And I just wanna say that I'm so sorry for everything, XL. I never should've told you I didn't want to stay married. You were right. I was pushing you away, and I shouldn't have. I should've been pulling you closer to me because that's what you do when you love someone. You pull them as close to your heart as you can, and you never fucking let go. I'm sorry I messed everything up between us and that I've been too scared to say this, but… I love you, Kendrick Patton. I love you more than anything, and I don't want to lose you to anyone else. Nothing is the same when you're not around. I want to stay married. I want to fix… whatever this is because I love it. I love us. Please, just… call me back and tell me what it is. Whatever you decide, I'll go with, but please consider giving us another c-chance."

My voice broke, and a sob escaped my lips as I hung up, feeling both emotionally freed and bound at the same time. I didn't know how something like that was even possible. I sank back into my pillow as both mental and physical exhaustion swept over me like an abrupt tidal wave. I closed my eyes, knowing I'd done all I could. All that was left to do was to pray he found it in his heart to love me past the pain I'd caused him.

XI

I was lying in my hotel bed, the time on my phone glowing 12:25 a.m. It vibrated in my hand with a notification of a new voice-mail. Instinctively, I opened it and listened, already knowing who it was from. I tapped the speaker button, and Zahra's sweet, familiar voice filled the room. She was worked up with emotion, but her apology and confession repeated in my brain long after the message ended.

I felt a knot in my chest. Perhaps it was my heart tugging at its reins, begging to break free from its icy entrapment, but I quickly brushed it aside. I had bigger shit to deal with than my broken heart and her bad timing. All I cared about was finding out who burned down my goddamned barbershop. Feeling more frustrated than senti-mental, I put my phone back on *Do Not Disturb*, wishing I could do the same for my emotions. I decided to sleep on it. As soon as I closed my eyes, the seed Amir planted about putting my pride aside and softening my heart lingered in my mind. But his words, no matter how influential, seemed empty now.

After tossing and turning for two hours, I finally gave up on finding sleep. The bed felt even colder without her by my side, and we hadn't slept next to each other in weeks. At two-something in the morning, I rolled out of bed, too restless to force my body to stay still. I headed down to the gym on the hotel's first floor, hoping a quick workout would help clear my mind or at least tire me out enough to where I'd go back upstairs and pass right out.

The clanking weights and rhythmic sounds of my shoes thumping against the treadmill did nothing to ease my unrest. After an hour in the gym, I headed to the twenty-four-hour convenience store near the front desk and charged a refrigerated smoothie to my room. When I got back upstairs, I paced, drank, and listened to Zahra's voicemail repeatedly until I felt the walls start closing in.

Each time I replayed it, her words chipped away at the safeguard I'd placed around my heart. Still, the rage and uncertainty over the barbershop fire annoyingly lingered over me like a dark cloak, and I allowed my bruised ego to overshadow my bruised heart. I hated choosing between the urgency of finding the truth and the raw, unguarded emotion her message stirred inside me.

I leaned back against the bed, staring up at the ceiling. The answers, my next move, the peace I sought from my spinning thoughts—none of it seemed within reach. The only thing that seemed tangible was her. And that was it. My mind was made up. I was going to get my wife.

THE NEXT THING I KNEW, I WAS DRESSED AND IN MY CAR, DAMN near breaking the speed limit to get across the city to the hospital. During the drive, all I kept thinking about was what I'd say when I saw her and what I'd do when those beautiful brown eyes locked on mine for the first time in over a week. I wasn't a simp, but I'd be a liar if I said I wasn't nervous as hell.

The hospital lobby was quiet as I approached the nurse's station. There was only one woman seated there. She had on a Garfield scrub top and wore long box braids cascading down her back.

"I'm here to see my wife," I announced. "Her name is Zahra Patton."

The nurse glanced at the clock and then back at me. "Sorry, sir. Visiting hours don't start again until eight o'clock," she said, almost regrettably.

Hell nah. That was four long hours away.

My heart sank, but I refused to be turned away. "I'm her husband," I asserted, my voice booming. "My wife needs me."

I stared at her, knowing she could see the determination in my pleading eyes. Before she could respond, I pulled out a roll of cash from my pocket, watching the crisp bills form a perfect cylinder. With a swift motion, I dropped it on the desk and let it roll toward her. The thick thud echoed slightly in the otherwise silent corridor.

"How much will it take for you to change your mind?" I probed.

The nurse's brown eyes never left the wad of cash. The longer she stared, the more I knew she was at a crossroads. For a minute, everything felt frozen in time.

The nurse hesitated but eventually nodded. She sighed hard while glancing around to ensure no one else was watching. "Okay," she whispered, scooping the money roll off the desk and tucking it discreetly into her scrub pocket before her nails started tapping away at the keyboard. "But you didn't get this from me. She's in room three-seventy-one. Hurry up and go."

I dipped my chin in gratitude before hurrying down the hallway toward the elevator. The door was slightly ajar when I reached her room. Seeing her sleeping peacefully tugged at my heartstrings, causing me to stop and stare. I gently pushed it open and stepped inside. There, on the hospital bed, lay Zahra, her eyes closed and her face solemn but peaceful and still as beautiful as ever. I crossed the room in a few strides and swallowed her hand in mine. The coolness of her soft skin sent a shiver rolling down my spine, and the softness of my touch caused her to stir in her slumber.

Her eyes fluttered open, and she looked momentarily confused. When she saw me, a flicker of surprise lit up her eyes.

"I heard your voicemail," I informed her.

Her breath caught in her chest as she looked away and yawned. "You did?"

I nodded solemnly. "Honestly, I wasn't sure if you'd be happy to see me."

She shot me a half-smirk before placing her other hand on mine. "I don't want to see anyone else."

The warmth of her touch sent a strange sensation rolling through me amid the tension between us. "Even at four in the mornin'?"

"Especially at four in the morning."

Then, our conversation started. It was exploratory, at first, about why she was back in the hospital so soon after her surgery. She informed me about the infection of her incision but assured me she was on the mend with the antibiotics the doctors had administered. Then, the conversation shifted to our feelings and all the fears and hopes that lay between our decision to stay married.

"What if I still die?" she asked, voice trembling.

"What if you live?" I suggested, offering her a brighter outlook on things.

My question lingered in the air as I squeezed her hand and looked into her eyes with a level of sincerity that shattered the glass castles we'd both built around our hearts.

"I love you, Zahra Patton. I've felt alone all my life until you came along. I meant what I told you in the hospital that day. You're mine, and I'm never letting you go."

Her eyes filled with tears as she reached up to cup the side of my face in her palm. "I love you too."

Both of us leaned in, and our lips met in a passionate kiss—eye boogers and morning breath be damned. For the first time in a long while, it felt like the beginning of healing, a fresh step toward our new future. I'd gotten my girl back, and that was all that mattered.

Zahra

I woke up the following day feeling like I'd lost my bearings, but I was soothed by the sight of XL still by my bedside, his thick beard pressed to his chest, and he snored softly. A smile inched up one side of my face, and I couldn't help but feel grateful. I gently stroked the skull tattoo on his hand as I watched his chest rise and fall.

Our perfect, peaceful moment was interrupted by a knock on the door. Although soft, it was still an unwanted intrusion into our bubble. XL shot to his feet, groggily rubbing his eyes as Doctor Ritter entered the room. She greeted us with a quirk of her lips before delivering the unexpectedly good news that the antibiotics were working and my latest lab results looked good enough to allow me to go home, provided that I continued with the medication for another week and changed the bandages on my incision at least twice a day.

I swept a happy tear from my eye. "Thank you so much, doctor!" I exclaimed, my relief evident in my tone.

With Doctor Ritter's official clean bill of health, it felt like a massive weight had been finally lifted off of me. XL helped me get dressed and gather my things, and we left the hospital hand-in-hand.

As we stepped outside, feeling the bright sun beating down on the pavement, XL halted and turned to face me with a smile leaning on half of his mouth.

"Let's go home, Mrs. Patton."

———

XL's phone vibrated with a text as we walked through the door. His eyes darted from left to right, reading the message to himself before sharing it with me. Sienna was in labor, and she and her husband were on their way to the hospital for the birth of their daughter.

My heart fluttered with delight for their family, but I felt an even greater joy returning home with XL by my side. I'd never been more grateful for a second chance in life and with the man I loved.

"That's so exciting! Did they pick out a name?"

"I think it's going to be Amira."

"That's pretty."

"Not as pretty as you, though."

I playfully rolled my eyes before looking at the sweatsuit, hospital socks, and Nike slides on my feet. "You'll say anything, won't you?"

"Only the truth."

"Yeah, well, this beauty is going to take a shower," I announced.

He offered to cook something for us, but I only craved his presence. We had the entire evening to relax, reconnect, and watch movies or some trash reality TV. I told him I wanted him all to myself and suggested ordering a couple of pizzas instead, even though I knew I was supposed to be eating small meals. His lips danced around a smile as he agreed.

"You want me to find a movie or something?" he called out as I went down the hall to the bedroom.

"Yeah. Sounds good."

He responded to me, but I was already in the bathroom with the shower running and couldn't hear him. I closed the door, peeling my clothes off as soon as I got inside. I flung them all over the place hastily before glancing at my reflection. My hair was pulled into a bun on top of my head, with highlighted wisps escaping and framing my face nicely. I slowly peeled the bandage away from my incision and was grateful to see it looked a lot better than it did previously. The unattractive red spots and bruises that once populated my skin had faded, and I finally started to feel like myself again. I stepped inside the shower and immediately drew back. The hot water scalded me before I turned it down.

The frosted glass shower door opened as I lathered my body with soap, revealing XL. His eyes devoured my naked body, and unlike the last time, I didn't shy away.

"I asked you what kind of pizza you were in the mood for, but now I see you didn't hear me," he stated, eyes slowly drawing their way up to my eyes from my breasts.

I smirked. "I'm craving anything with lots of pepperoni! And maybe some Italian sausage too."

"Meat lovers pizza got it," he replied, although he didn't move a muscle.

"Anything else I can help you with?" I inquired, biting on my bottom lip.

He shot me a sexy smirk. "Nah. I got everything I needed. Anything I can help you with?"

"Maybe you could take care of this issue I've been having lately. This ache always seems to be present whenever I'm around you…"

"Where exactly is the ache?"

I turned to him and spread my legs by propping up one leg on the Roman shower seat. "Right here," I answered, pointing to my pussy.

"Are you sure you're up to it?" he asked, eyeing my incision.

I looked down at my yoni, then back up at him before slipping my hand between my thighs. "She sure is."

"Say less."

He stepped back suddenly and pulled off his shirt, revealing a husky torso covered in tattoos that led to an enticing trail that disappeared into his pants. His hand reached out to replace mine as he cupped my center. I moaned softly as his fingertips danced circles around my clit before he plunged two fingers inside, curling them to hit that sweet spot. One hand palmed the shower wall while my other cupped my right breast, gently teasing my nipple between my fingers. Panting, I tilted my head back with a quiet groan, letting the water pelt my skin as he finger fucked me.

I purred. "Mmm shit, baby. Don't stop."

"That's it, cum all over daddy's fingers."

As I neared climax, my hips began to move instinctively, pressing into his touch. I bit down on my lip to muffle another moan as pleasure surged through me unexpectedly. Gasping, I felt a wave of ecstasy ripple through me, causing my knees to weaken.

"Oooh fuck," I squealed, drawing in quick, wispy breaths. "Don't stop. Don't stop."

Increasing the speed and pressure of his movements, XL found the perfect rhythm that pushed me over the edge into another realm of bliss. A silent scream escaped my parted lips as I climaxed intensely, feeling the walls of my core contract around his fingers.

"That's it. That's a good girl," he whispered against my wet, soapy skin.

As good as I felt, our foreplay didn't help my urges. If anything, it made them worse. All I could picture was him fucking me from behind while he pressed on my clit. God, how badly I wanted to feel him. I knew he was only holding back because I was still recovering from my surgery and was advised to stay away from strenuous activities. I wanted to sob from the ache that was still present and had half a mind to tell him to fuck me anyway, but I knew I had to rest my body.

With a half-contented sigh, I allowed him to finish washing me up and stepped out of the shower. XL handed me a plush towel and gently dried me off, patting my incision dry before rebandaging it.

"What's wrong?" he inquired, looking up at me. "You look too sad for a woman who just creamed down my hand."

I sighed heavily, unable to hide my frustration, sexually and otherwise. "I wanna feel you."

"I know."

"Right now," I whined. "I hate that you can't touch me like I want you to."

He hesitated a moment before his eyes darkened, and he closed the slither of space between his chest and mine. "Who says I can't touch you?"

And then his lips were on mine, a searing passion, an ache burning through me and lighting my yoni on fire. The warmth of his breath was on my lips as his strong hands gently cupped my face, pulling me into him. Our kiss deepened, and I moaned into it. His tongue danced with mine, teasing and demanding, his firm body gently pressed against me. His lips were full and soft. They moved in a way that made me want him to put them somewhere else. Somewhere lower. I melted into him, feeling the hardness of his chest against the softness of mine.

When he pulled away for air, I could barely catch my breath. My heart raced as he looked down at me, his eyes dark with lust. He ran his fingers over my cheek, trailing them down my neck and across my collarbone.

"You are so fucking beautiful," he whispered hoarsely. "And those eyes... damn, Zahra."

His hands traveled lower to rest on my hips as he squeezed, almost as if trying to stop himself from what he was about to do.

My mouth watered as he reached for my towel and slowly lifted it over my thighs, exposing more of my legs to the warm, damp air in the bathroom.

"I can't lie," he said, glancing down at the bulge in his pants. "You got my dick harder than Chinese arithmetic right now. Tell me to stop, and I will."

I bit my lip and nodded, knowing he wouldn't receive an objection from me. I leaned against the nearest wall for support to prevent my legs from betraying me the moment he touched my sweet spot again.

His fingers brushed against my center, and I held back a gasp. He smirked wickedly before leaning in to capture my lips in another searing kiss that sent a spark straight to my core.

His hands roamed up the inside of my thighs, causing goosebumps to form as they made their way higher toward their ultimate destination.

I held onto him tighter, my pussy clenching as I waited. The anticipation built within me as he traced circles around my entrance, making me squirm for more. And then, finally—he slipped a finger into me, exploring my wetness with unnerving skillfulness. A moan escaped from deep within me at the feeling.

The room seemed to spin a little as another finger slipped inside me. It felt so good yet so wrong at the same time. But I didn't give a fuck. I wanted him. I wanted more. His thumb circled that achingly sensitive bud while another finger stretched me open wider amidst deep throaty moans escaping from between clenched teeth.

"Shit, that pussy is so fuckin' wet."

I couldn't take it anymore, and I moaned, "Please, Kendrick, fuck me. I can't... I can't take it any longer."

"Mmmm, soon." He slid his fingers out of me, licking them off with a seductive growl. "Fucking delicious. Move your sexy ass over to the bed and lay down."

On shaky legs, I obeyed, walking into the bedroom and lying on the bed. My legs fell open, spreading wide like a starfish. He joined me on the bed, sticking his fingers back inside me and finger fucking me so quickly that the build-up came hot and heavy.

"Oh my God. I'm gonna cum," I managed to whimper just as he twisted his fingers and I squirted, my juices flowing down my legs and dripping onto the bed that hadn't been made since I'd left the day before.

"You look so good when you cum."

He leaned down to kiss my pussy before I heard the sound of a zip. I watched eagerly as he pushed his pants and boxers down to his ankles, freeing his huge, thick dick. The sudden sight of him made me gasp. Fuck, I wanted it so damn bad.

"I'ma go nice and easy, okay? Don't you move a muscle."

I nodded. With a low groan, he pressed the thick tip of his dick against my dripping entrance, rubbing up and down my slit before easing inside, filling me up in one slow stroke. He hovered over me and sucked on my neck, nipping lightly as he began to curve his hips to fuck me at a gentle pace. It felt incredible.

I hissed out a breath as he pulled back, grazing his teeth across my shoulder blade. "Fuck," I heard him mutter as he hit my cervix, still holding back from fucking me harder. "You feel so good."

He reached for my breasts, his strong hands tweaking and squeezing just right to make me beg for more. Each thrust sent shock-waves through my body as I bit down on my lip to muffle the cries of pleasure that threatened to escape.

He gently eased my right leg around his waist, and I was suddenly aching for more. "Yes, Kendrick, baby! Just like that." I moaned quietly between gasps for air. His name would forever be on my lips.

He obliged, turning me into a ball of need and lust. My throbbing clit tingled from the friction that caused sparks of pleasure to shoot straight to it with every long, slow stroke. *God, this man knows exactly what he's doing to me.*

"You take this dick so good, baby," he groaned as he pushed into me further, his length hitting impossibly deep with each passionate thrust.

My muffled moans and soft whimpers were enough to have him fuck me deeper. I moaned in ecstasy as he picked up the pace while his other hand reached between our bodies to worship my clit. The combination was too much, making me beg for release. My walls clenched around him with each thrust, feeling incredible. The last thing on my mind was my incision. All I cared about was my release.

"Oh my God," I cried out, trying to stop my hips from eagerly meeting his every movement. He leaned forward so that his face was level with mine, nipping at my bottom lip and sucking on my tongue.

"Say it," he whispered against my lips.

"I want to cum, baby."

"Drip all over this dick, baby. It's yours."

And the floodgates opened. It was as if he'd said a magic incantation over my pussy. His hips slapped into me with an unhurried but firm pace, his dick hitting my cervix as he bottomed out, and my body gave in. My orgasm tore through me with a long, drawn-out moan.

"Oh fuck, fuck…"

"Mmm, shit," he growled before he came inside me, neglecting to pull out in time to bust, but I didn't care. I was still trying to ride my own orgasmic wave.

Panting, he collapsed next to me as my legs vibrated with aftershocks. "So," he mumbled into my ear, running his hands along my soaked thighs. He let out a low chuckle as his fingers played with my clit, the sensation putting me into overload. "Such a pretty pussy. So glad you're mine so that I can wear that pussy out again later."

My eyes rolled back as he pinched slightly before releasing, "Mmmm, okay, but you gotta feed me first. I'm suddenly starving, and my stomach is feigning for a slice of pizza, even if I only take one bite."

He leaned in to kiss my sweaty forehead. "Sounds like a plan, baby girl."

Hours later, we were cuddled up on the couch enjoying a movie and the warmth of each other's company when XL's phone buzzed with a text.

"Amira's here," he announced with a smile while flashing the screen toward me.

It was a picture of his cousin's new bundle of joy. She was a beautiful baby girl with bright caramel skin swaddled in a pink receiving blanket with a lock of jet-black hair poking out from underneath her snug baby hat. I beamed at the sight of her tiny features and precious face, feeling a wave of baby fever wash over me as I realized we might've made one of our own hours prior.

"She's gorgeous. I'm so happy for them."

XL nodded as his eyes twinkled with joy. It was the first time in a long time I'd seen him so genuinely happy. "Me too. Maybe we can visit them tomorrow if you're feeling up to it. Besides, it's way past time for me to formally introduce you to my cousins, who are more like my brothers."

"We can do that. But for now, I'm just glad to be here with you," I declared, resting my head against his bare chest. "This is exactly what I needed. You feel like home."

He wrapped his strong arm around me and gently kissed the top of my head as we refocused our attention back on the movie. "So do you, Zahra. So do you."

THE FOLLOWING DAY, I WOKE UP FEELING REFRESHED AND excited to meet XL's family officially. We dressed and ate breakfast before heading to the hospital to join the rest of the Patton crew and bask in the joy of welcoming the new baby.

Clutching the teddy bear and welcome baby balloons in my grasp, I stepped into Sienna's hospital room, unsure of what awaited me on the other side. Sienna was resting in her hospital bed, cradling her newborn daughter to her chest. Her husband, Ahsan, sat beside her, his face filled with bliss and awe as he gazed at his two girls as if they were the only women in the world. I knew that look. It was the same way XL looked at me. That's all it took to tell that Sienna was truly loved, which only made me happier for her.

Kendrick grinned widely as he approached the bed with me a couple of steps behind. "Hey, there. Look at that beauty. She's a real-life angel! Congratulations, you two! I'm so happy for you both."

He stepped aside, revealing me standing in his shadow. A nervous smirk crawled up my face, unsure of how they'd react to my presence. I didn't know it was possible to feel like family and an outsider at the same time. Luckily, I was ambushed with welcoming smiles and well wishes from his cousins and their girls for my continued good health. I figured everyone was too enamored with the new baby to grill me about why I lied about being the housekeeper or why I was still alive in the first place. A win was a win, and I'd take it with no questions asked.

I placed the teddy bear and balloons on the side table. "You did so well, Sienna. She's perfection wrapped up in one tiny little body. The name Amira fits her well. I know things have been weird with us, but I am so happy for you."

"Thank you, Zahra. That means a lot."

I dipped my chin. "Don't mention it."

"I'm not trying to take all the credit," Amir inserted himself into our conversation. "But I was the one who put it out into the universe that if you two had a baby girl, you'd name her after her favorite uncle, and look what happened. I'm just sayin'."

XL chuckled before clearing his throat. "Everyone, I want to take a second to introduce you to my wife Zahra officially."

My knees began to feel wobbly, and I felt XL's strong arm slip around my waist to anchor me. His touch instantly soothed me and helped me find my words. "It's nice to meet you all finally," I said, my expression relaxing into a smile.

"Zahra, we've been looking forward to meeting you," Ahsan said.

"Cleaning lady, my ass." Amir scoffed. "Nah. I'm just playing. We've heard a lot about you. Mostly good things, I promise," Amir chimed in with a playful chuckle.

I blinked away the tears welling in my eyes, suddenly overwhelmed by their kind-heartedness. "I thought you all might be skeptical about me being here..."

"I'm all about love today, and as long as you're making our boy happy, you're good with me. That's all I've ever wanted for him," Ahsan assured me with sincerity.

"Yeah, he's always been there for us. The nigga deserves all the happiness in the world. I never knew the nigga had such nice teeth before you came along. Nigga never used to show teeth, and now you got my man cheesin' like a kid in a candy store," Amir revealed.

His brother chuckled. "Exactly. Family means everything to us, and you're a part of that now."

"Welcome to the Patton family, Zahra," Amir confirmed, reaching out to hug his cousin and then me.

"Thank you, truly. I didn't expect such a warm welcome given our initial meeting."

"It was a lot warmer than the welcome I got," Sienna joked. "They must really like you."

A woman holding a baby boy with a few teeth in his mouth stepped forward to introduce herself. "And I'm Nerissa, Amir's wife. And this is baby Eli. I can't wait to get to know you better."

"Thank you all so much. I'm truly grateful to be a part of this family."

"See, I told you they'd love you." XL beamed, springing a grin.

I felt my heart expand two times its size. His formal introduction of me as his wife was more than a check off his to-do list; it was his heartfelt declaration to the people he loved that I was truly a part of his family.

An hour passed, and the room was still filled with laughter and chatter as everyone shared stories and funny memories while taking turns passing around the baby. The longer we stayed, the more I felt our bond growing stronger. It was a moment of camaraderie I'd missed since the loss of my brother. Being around them made me realize that family wasn't just about blood ties but the support and compassion it took to build a lasting foundation—something special. I couldn't help but feel a new lease on life and an unrivaled level of gratitude for my clean bill of health and the love that enveloped me.

"Come on, y'all, let's pose for a pic," Amir suggested.

All of us posed for a family photo, capturing the special moment. Amir set the timer on his phone and snapped a few pictures before promptly posting them online, sharing his brother's happiness with the world.

XL leaned in to kiss my cheek gently. "I'll be right back."

He stepped out of the room to take a phone call. I approached the window near the door and watched him pace up and down the hallway with his phone glued to his ear. Instantly, I noticed the sudden shift in his jovial expression. Whatever the phone call was about, it wasn't good news and could potentially rain on everyone's fucking parade.

My phone vibrated in my pocket, urging me to answer it. I stepped away from Sienna's hospital room until the laughter and conversations from inside were drowned out. The hallway on the maternity floor was mostly quiet, allowing me to focus on the person on the other line. It was one of my hittas named Bones. I took a deep breath, knowing the call could bring the news I'd anxiously awaited for weeks.

"Yeah, I'm here," I answered firmly.

"I'm sorry to call knowing y'all got all the family shit going on today, but this can't wait."

"You got a name for me?"

His voice was low and serious. "His name is Jack Davis, and he goes by Jack the Trap on the streets because, apparently, he's a jack of all trades. Mothafucka will wash your car, shine your shoes, and offer to watch your fuckin' baby, all for a quick fix. He's a fuckin' junkie and the one who set fire to your barbershop."

My jaw tightened. "You sure?"

"Positive. One of my regulars told me he recently overheard him in the alley talkin' about trying to scrape up some cash so he could get out of Vegas because niggas were on his head about the fire."

"You got his location?"

"We can grab him. Just say when."

"Snatch his ass up, and bring him to the warehouse. Call me when it's done."

"Understood," he replied without hesitation. "We'll handle it."

I gripped the phone tighter, with devious thoughts dancing through my head. "Good. Make sure he's ready to talk."

I paused after ending the call, taking a few seconds to compose myself before re-entering Sienna's hospital room. I was torn between the joy of Ahsan's new addition and the need for justice for the fire that destroyed part of my livelihood. I knew I had to hide it from Ahsan as best as possible, at least for now. I stepped back inside with my face a mask of calm and caught Amir's eye. I subtly waved him over, and we walked back into the hallway.

I leaned in with a low, urgent whisper. "Amir, I just got a call. They found the mothafucka who set fire to my barbershop."

Amir's eyes ballooned before his relaxed expression turned serious. "What you wanna do?"

"I've instructed Bones and the hittas to capture him and bring him to the warehouse. I want to question him myself."

Amir nodded in understanding. "All right."

"But we can't tell Ahsan. Not today. I don't want to stain the day his child was born with the blood of my enemy."

Amir agreed. "You're right. We'll handle this quietly. He doesn't need to be involved right now."

"How quickly can you wrap things up here? I know you wanna make sure Nerissa and Eli are good."

Amir nodded about to speak, just as Zahra found and approached us.

"Everything good, baby?" she asked, searching my eyes for the truth.

"I'ma let y'all talk," Amir confirmed. "I'll catch up with you in a minute."

I closed the gap between us and took her by the hand. "I'm good."

"You're lying. I can see the rage in your eyes."

Before I could inform her about what happened, her attention was diverted over my shoulder. She stepped around me, eyes narrowing on a woman I hadn't seen before.

"What are you doing here?" she asked, her voice firm but calm.

The woman crossed her arms defiantly. "Can't tell a bitch with a new job when you see one?" she replied, flaunting the burgundy scrubs she wore.

"I'm being serious, Zyon. Today isn't the day for your bullshit. How about you go do whatever job you have here."

I paused, looking the woman up and down with a grimace. I'd finally laid eyes on Zyon, and she was nothing special. She reeked of cigarette smoke, and her burgundy-colored box braids were as over-grown as her long, acrylic fingernails. The only thing she had going for her was that she had a job at the hospital, but the bitch wasn't no doctor, so I could give a fuck less.

"My bullshit? Sienna is *my* cousin. I have every right to be here and see my family."

"This is a special moment for her, and I'm not about to let you ruin it just like you ruin everything else. How did you even know she had the baby?"

"I saw the photo she posted online. There. Happy now? Now, move!"

"I'm not letting you go in there if she doesn't know you're coming. You're poison, Zyon. You ruin everything you touch."

"That's my fuckin' cousin, bitch!" the woman declared loudly.

The sudden escalation in her voice made me step to Zahra's side, my expression serious as I took a protective stance. "Do we have a fuckin' problem here?"

I wasn't the only one who'd heard the commotion because soon enough, Nerissa and Amir barreled out of Sienna's room to see what was happening. Their expressions turned from curiosity to alertness. Whatever joyous atmosphere we had had been frozen in time and replaced with thick tension.

Nerissa raced forward, raising her voice with anger and protectiveness. "I thought the last time I saw you, I told you to stay the fuck away."

The woman smirked, her voice dripping with false sweetness. "I'm here to see my cousin and her new baby. Is that a problem?"

"It absolutely is."

"Don't you have somebody's edges to pull out? Oops, I mean style."

Nerissa's eyes narrowed to slits as she processed Zyon's fighting words. The bitch must've had a death wish talkin' crazy about her hair business, especially when Amir was around. It instantly hit a nerve, and suddenly, Nerissa cocked her head to the side.

"Hold up. All those fake ass one-star reviews on my business page, the negative comments—it was you this entire time trying to sabotage my business, wasn't it?"

Zyon chuckled. "I can't take credit for initiating the drag of you online, but I won't deny participating in it. I couldn't help myself."

Nerissa took a step closer, squeezing her hands into fists, and Amir stepped in stride right along with her, ready to ride. "Bitch, are you crazy? You're fuckin' with my livelihood," Nerissa growled, her voice hushed and controlled, careful not to draw any more unwanted attention to us.

Zyon rolled her neck, emphasizing her response. "That's what you get for fucking threatening me."

"Bitch, I oughta—"

Amir stepped in front of his wife in an attempt to put an end to their bickering before Nerissa put holy hands on the woman. His voice boomed as he spoke. "It's clear you're not fuckin' welcome here. This is a family celebration, so why don't you fuckin' beat it before shit gets hectic up in here."

"Are you fucking threatening me?"

Nerissa hopped back into the argument, her tone serious as she poked her head around the wall Amir had made in front of her. "You need to leave, Zyon! Take your thieving ass and go. Sienna doesn't want to see you. You lucky I haven't told her what you did, but just because I didn't tell her, doesn't mean I didn't tell them that you set up that robbery with my brother to rob your own family," she revealed.

"You heard them," Zahra added. "Turn around and go."

"I don't know what you're talking about, and I'm not going anywhere! I'm an employee and have every right to see my cousin and her child!"

"Not today, bitch. Leave before we report your ass for harassment and get you fired," Nerissa threatened.

The four of us stood united, blocking her path and trying to handle the situation before she woke the bear and Ahsan popped out of the room. I knew all hell would break loose then.

Moments later, two hospital security guards arrived. They quickly moved to escort Zyon off the maternity floor despite her protests that she was an employee and had every right to be there. It turns out that she worked on the first floor in medical billing. It finally sunk in that she was outnumbered, outmatched, and seconds away from getting sent home.

As Zyon was led back to her floor by hospital security, we breathed a sigh of relief. We stood there until she was out of sight, then returned to the room. I snaked my arm around Zahra's waist, giving her a reassuring squeeze. Watching her go so hard to protect my family's peace only solidified our bond and commitment.

We hung back. Now that I'd seen Zyon's messy ass in person, I couldn't help but want to know the backstory between her and Zahra. Whatever the story was, I knew it couldn't be good.

I chuckled, half kidding, half serious. "I see why you said she makes your ass itch. That bitch is a piece of work."

Zahra rolled her eyes. "Tell me about it."

"She's gone now. You don't have to worry about her anymore."

"Good."

"What's your issue with her anyway? You never did tell me."

Zahra's jaw muscles firmed into a rigid line, and pain fogged her eyes before she finally spoke. "You remember I told you about my twin brother, right?"

I dipped my chin. "Yeah, Lorenzo."

"Zyon and I used to be thick as thieves. We did everything together, from wearing each other's clothes to crushing on the same boys. Everything changed when she started dating Zo behind my back. I could feel something was off, but I couldn't put my finger on it. But this nagging feeling in my gut told me something wasn't right. She started clutching her phone extra tight and being all secretive whenever I was around or started wearing skimpier and skimpier things whenever she came over, and she knew my brother was home.

"Zo suddenly became obsessed with how good his body looked and smelled, and he always talked low on the phone to someone in his room late at night. Their secret continued for months before I finally put two and two together. To make matters worse, I caught her fucking on somebody else that lived in the neighborhood across the tracks. She confessed it had been going on for almost as long as she'd been dating Zo. Everything got weird and messy between us after I told her she needed to tell him or I would."

"And did she?"

She rolled her eyes. "Of course, she didn't. The ho skated off to Miami and never looked back."

"Damn. That's fucked up."

"Not only did I lose my best friend, but I also had to be the one to see my brother pick his broken heart up off the ground. He'd never admitted it to me, but I think Zyon was his first love, which only pisses me off even more. She doesn't deserve to hold a special place in his life. I wish she could be as simple as a photo memory in my camera roll that I could delete."

"I feel that. It had to be tough."

"It was. In the beginning, I was in denial. I didn't want to believe that my best friend could betray me and my brother. But as it turned out, if she could do it to me, she could do it to anybody. Even when you wanna see the good in them, some bitches are just born nasty, I guess."

"So, you don't think she ever cared about him?"

"If she did, she had a funny way of showing it. The part that pissed me off the most was knowing that I ignored my instincts. If I'd leaned into my suspicions more and trusted my gut in the beginning, maybe I could've talked some sense into him and steered him away from her clutches."

"I mean, you can't help who you fall for, but isn't it one of the ten commandments that say not to fuck with your sibling's best friend?"

My joke brought a flicker of humor to her eyes, causing them to crinkle at the sides as she pulled a slow smile. "That's what I'm saying. The bitch had zero home training."

"I can tell."

"From that moment forward, I vowed never to fall prey to another Miami ho's schemes again. Since then, I've kept everybody at arm's length."

"Except me," I confirmed.

"Yeah. You're the only exception to the rule."

I smirked. "I'm honored."

"You oughta be. We should get back in there before they come looking for us."

"Okay, but listen, Amir and I are going to ride out and handle some business soon. Do you want to stay here with Sienna and Nerissa until we come back or head home?"

"How long is this ride of yours going to take?"

"I'm not sure," I answered to the best of my ability.

Zahra took a deep breath and sighed it out.

"I'll stay here for now. If you think it'll be another hour, I'll call an Uber home or something."

"You sure?" I inquired, having second thoughts about leaving her side.

"Yeah. I am."

"Okay."

"Listen to me," she said, pulling my hand before I could reach for the hospital door. "Whatever it is you gotta do, just make sure you come back to me in one piece, deal?"

"Deal," I replied, sealing my promise with a kiss.

We returned to the hospital room, grateful that Ahsan and Sienna's celebration of the birth of their child had remained untarnished by all the unexpected hostility in the hallway. I chiseled a smile into my features and sat tight until I heard from Bones. Because when I did, it would be on.

———

AMIR AND I ARRIVED AT THE DIMLY LIT WAREHOUSE AN HOUR later with our guns. We marched inside and stood over the man who had confessed to setting fire to my barbershop as he sat tied to a chair, looking like a junkie in need of his next fix. His brown skin had an ashy overtone, and from the white around his dried, flaky lips, he was severely dehydrated and possibly malnourished. Bones was right. The mothafucka was a junkie. He looked like the type to steal your packages off your doorstep and try to sell the shit back to you. Only, I didn't know who he was, but I was determined to find out.

I slid on my fitted gloves before putting on my brass knuckles. "Who the fuck are you, and why the fuck did you burn down my barbershop, nigga?" I growled before landing a powerful blow to his jaw and sending two of his yellowed teeth sliding across the floor.

"Speak, or I'll take the rest of your teeth out of your dirty fuckin' mouth one by one."

His eyes darted from left to right, bouncing around his fucking head like a ping-pong ball. "P-please, I haven't slept in days."

My frustration continued to grow as he squirmed and moaned in pain but relayed no helpful information. That's when I noticed the marks on his arms from shooting up with needles. Sweat poured down his forehead, and he kept grinding his teeth while making jerky movements, although he was restrained to the chair. He was tweaking out on meth, heroin, or something of the sort.

"Pliers," I instructed.

Amir stood behind me with a devious smirk and the pliers in hand. "Open wide, mothafucka."

He gripped the man's jaw and leaned over him with the pliers, ready to attack.

"Okay, okay. I'll talk," the man cried out, chest heaving in and out as his body continued to shake.

"Why the fuck did you burn down my shop?" I asked again, fists balled with rage.

"I was paid to do it."

"Paid in what, and by who?" Amir yelled out before clamping the pliers down on the man's left ear, instantly crushing all three bones.

"Ahh shit!" he hissed, seconds away from losing consciousness. "S-some bitch named Z-Zyon I met outside the strip club. She said she had a hookup at a hospital and could get me drugs. You know, the real good shit."

I knew a fuckin' fiend when I saw one, and I knew junkies would do just about anything to get their next fix. They didn't require rhyme or reason to complete a task as long as there was a pot of drugs at the end of the rainbow.

I leaned in closer, my voice filled with rage. "Tell me why the fuck Zyon wanted my barbershop destroyed. What was her fuckin' motive?"

The man wagged his head back and forth, looking afraid as his eyes bounced around the space, but still defiant. "I told you everything I know. She paid me to do a job. That's it."

Amir took the pliers to the man's other ear, sticking to his torture approach. "Think harder, bitch nigga. Your life's on the line. There has to be something else. What exactly did she say to you?"

Blood was leaking out of both sides of the man's head. I still wasn't satisfied. "Verbatim, mothafucka."

"I swear, that's all I know. I didn't get the details, mothafucka! All I got were the drugs and the money to buy and fill up the gas can!"

Amir and I exchanged a look of frustration. We know he was only a small piece of the puzzle, and we needed more information to understand Zyon's true motives and protect the people we loved. I released the safety on my gun, past the point of showing the mothafucka mercy. He did a job, and he'd have to suffer the consequences for doing so. There was no remorse in my heart for him. I was ready to waste that nigga.

I aimed my gun at the center of his forehead while resting my finger on the trigger. I drew in and released a deep breath before popping the trigger three times and sending him to meet his maker.

Amir and I left the warehouse and returned to the hospital, riding in tense silence and hoping Zyon was still on the clock. As I sped down the road gripping the steering wheel, I was sure my cousin's mind was racing with as many questions as mine was, trying to piece together the puzzle that just didn't make any fucking sense.

"How the fuck can some random bitch have beef with us when she doesn't even know us?" Amir wondered aloud.

I sat in silence for a second, pausing to let the gears in my brain turn for a minute or two more before responding. "She doesn't have to know us personally to hate us. Nobody is immune from hate. It's poison. Besides, something tells me we're not the issue here."

Amir glanced over at me with a puzzled look on his face. "What do you mean?"

I shifted uncomfortably in my seat while connecting the dots. "Think about it. First, she staged the break-in and robbed her own cousin. Then, the gallery where Sienna's artwork was showcased got vandalized with that cryptic ass message. Soon after that, the barbershop fire occurred, and she admitted to making those false rumors online and trying to sabotage Nerissa's hair business. All roads point to our women. This shit isn't about us directly at all. She's coming for us through them."

Amir frowned. "Why just you and not Ahsan and me too?"

My shoulders rose and fell. "I don't know. Maybe because Zahra hasn't established anything out here yet? But there's something bigger at play here. I can feel that shit in my bones, nigga. We need to find that bitch Zyon and get to the bottom of this tonight."

The tension remained high as Amir and I continued our ride to the hospital, determined to find Zyon and uncover the truth. With so much uncertainty surrounding me, one thing was clear: We'd stop at nothing to protect our family and seek vengeance for the wrongs committed against us. I pulled into the expansive hospital parking lot, driving slowly through the parked cars, looking for any sign of Zyon since we knew she worked there.

"There that bitch go right there," Amir called out, spotting Zyon standing outside one of the hospital exits, her cigarette smoke curling into the air.

We exchanged heated looks and silently agreed on our plan of attack. I halted, allowing him time to jump out so we could split up to catch her ass off guard.

"I'll run up to her. You be ready to pull up," Amir confirmed.

I nodded. "Bet. Let's get this fuckin' bitch."

Amir swiftly approached Zyon, closing the distance between them within seconds. I pulled the car behind her as she turned to see who was coming. In a swift, coordinated move, Amir grabbed Zyon and forced her into the vehicle's back seat. She struggled, but she was no match for his unbreakable force. One blow to the head, and she was out cold.

BACK AT THE WAREHOUSE, I CARRIED ZYON'S BODY INSIDE, THEN Amir tied her to a chair. The space was tense, with everyone waiting to see how things would play out. She sat there, her body slumped over and unconscious. A bucket of water sat nearby, ready to be used.

"Time to wake this bitch up," I growled.

Amir and I exchanged knowing glances before he lifted the bucket and splashed the cold water over her face. She jerked awake, sputtering and gasping for air.

I paced in front of her, my voice cold. "Wake the fuck up, bitch." I wasted no time leaning in, my voice ice cold as I questioned her. "Why the fuck did you hire someone to burn down my barbershop?"

She blinked rapidly, trying to regain her bearings. "What... I don't know what the fuck you're talking about!"

Amir stepped closer with a menacing tone dripping from his lips. "Don't play dumb now, bitch. We already know you're behind it. The nigga you paid to do it already gave your ass up."

"So, why the fuck did you do it, Zyon? Why get somebody to set fire to my barbershop?"

"Let me the fuck go! I have to get back to work."

"Getting fired should be the least of your worries," I barked.

She glared at me defiantly, her voice dripping with sarcasm. "You think I'm going to just tell you, nigga? Fuck you! Fuck all of you!"

Amir grunted. "We ain't got all night, bitch. Start talking. Now."

"Fuck it. You wanna know why I burned down your shit? It's all because of Demario. I wanted revenge for what happened to him! He didn't deserve to go out like that."

My brows snapped together in confusion, my anger flaring through my nostrils. "What the fuck does Demario have to do with this? Why target me? I didn't kill that mothafucka!" I roared.

"I know. Ahsan did. I saw him," she revealed.

My eyes popped wide. "What the fuck did you just say?"

"Fuckin' liar!" Amir declared.

"Fuck you! I'm telling the truth," she spat back, her voice trembling with rage. "I was the one who dropped Demario off at his sister's apartment the day he got shot, but I never left. I parked and was on my phone waiting for him to call me and tell me to come back to get him when I heard the gunshots ring out and saw the car that pulled away. I know exactly what the fuck I saw. Ahsan was the one in the driver's seat."

My expression went blank. "You saw him?" I asked, my voice barely above a whisper.

Zyon nodded. "Yes, I fucking saw him! I know exactly what the nigga looks like. And ever since that day, I've wanted to make every single last one of you pay. Your fucking family took someone I cared about, and I wasn't going to let that shit go unanswered."

Amir and I exchanged another glance. Zyon's leak about Ahsan's involvement in Demario's death hit my ears like a ton of bricks. As her words continued to sink in, the puzzle pieces started to come together faster. I couldn't believe Ahsan had taken Demario out without telling us, but then again, I guess we all had our secrets.

Amir pressed further. "Sienna is your fuckin' blood. Why the fuck would you choose to avenge another nigga over her?"

"Because he was more family to me than Sienna could ever be! Demario didn't deserve to go out like that, laid out in the fuckin' street like roadkill. And then when that bitch Nerissa started talking crazy to me at the cemetery, threatening me and shit when all I did was come there to pay respects to her brother!" she yelled with hot tears pumping out of her eyes.

"Watch your fuckin' mouth behind my wife, bitch," Amir scolded her.

"Nigga, fuck your wife! Everybody was so caught up with putting together the pieces to their perfect little lives with all the fucking baby announcements, engagements, and weddings! But what about mine, huh? Where's my happily ever after? Those bitches got every-thing, and I got nothing! So, I said fuck it and decided to make you all pay. Everybody always underestimated me, but look. One by one, I made all of your lives a living hell," she spat, her voice laced with bitterness.

The simmering anger inside me rose again as my face contorted into a deadly scowl. I was furious that her calculated thirst for vengeance had put our entire family in danger and disrupted our lives time and time again. It finally all made sense. Her hate campaign had tried to demolish our sanity piece by piece.

Amir and I must've gotten tired of hearing her speak at the same time because we both drew our guns on her, fingers itching to pull the trigger.

"Do you wanna do the honors, or should I?" Amir inquired as his eyes darted over to mine.

"Man, fuck this bitch. I say we run a murder train on this ho and blow her brains out at the same goddamn time," I growled.

He shrugged nonchalantly. "Works for me."

"Bet."

Pow! Pow! Pow! Pow! Pow!

I continued to fire bullets into her until my gun was empty. I looked at the slumped body before us. Her blood was pooled around the chair, constantly dripping like a leaky faucet. Zyon was nothing but a delusional pawn, thinking she was a queen. She didn't deserve an ounce of our fuckin' mercy.

The night was far from over, but at least we had a clear picture of who our enemy was and the motive behind it all. I lowered my gun and tucked it in my pants before fully turning to face Amir.

"Call Ahsan. We need to talk, plus we're going to need more chemicals. It's time to make her and that tweaked-out mothafucka disappear for good."

———

Ahsan arrived with a pensive look on his face. He surveyed the scene before him—two dead bodies, bullet rounds, and a hell of a lot of blood.

"Do I even want to know what happened here?"

Amir stepped forward. "The bitch is Sienna's cousin Zyon, and the dead mothafucka beside her is the junkie she paid to burn down XL's shop."

"She was the one behind it all," I confirmed.

"Why'd she do it?"

"That bitch said she was the one that dropped Demario off at Nerissa's the day he got popped. Then, she tried to lie on you and say that you were the one who shot him. That shit ain't true, right?" Amir presumed.

I stepped forward amid Ahsan's silence. "Is it?" I probed.

Ahsan stared at us blankly for a few seconds before simply dipping his chin in acknowledgment. "Yeah. I killed him."

Amir's face opened wide with shock at his brother's emotionless confession. "What, nigga? It was *you* the whole time? Why the fuck didn't you tell me?"

"We both know why I didn't tell you, Amir. You're my brother. I couldn't let you take that L, and I'd do that shit again if I had to," he confirmed with zero remorse.

"Why? I told you I'd handle it."

"I know what you said."

"Then you should've fuckin' let me."

"We both know you couldn't. Your hands were tied, Amir, and that's okay. I took care of Demario, and y'all took care of Zyon. Looks like we're even to me. An enemy is an enemy. If they're no longer a threat, why does it matter who took their piece off the board?"

"It's the principle, nigga. My word should've been enough for you to stand the fuck down," Amir argued, wrinkled lines assembling on his forehead.

"I understand that, and that's exactly why that shit ate away at me for months. But the minute I stepped into that hospital room on the day my nephew was born, I knew I'd never be able to tell you. I'd never seen you that happy before. I knew I'd done the right thing. Demario was a threat to your family and mine. I had no choice but to fold that nigga."

My features drew tight with confusion. "What do you mean yours too?"

Ahsan's face carved into unforgiving lines. "Sienna confronted me about not telling her that I knew about Nerissa and Demario being brother and sister. The mothafucka had her so shaken up that she wanted to call off the wedding. I couldn't allow that to happen. Y'all know I'm not the type to ever let a mothafucka disrupt my life or make my girl uncomfortable, whether I'm in the game or not."

Ahsan was a testament that you could snatch the man out of the streets, but you'd never be able to siphon the streets out of the man.

He grunted as he looked down at Zyon's lifeless body. "I swear I didn't see any other car there waiting on him. She must've moved her car or circled back around without me noticing. I kept my eyes lasered in on her apartment the whole time and left the engine running, ready to pop his head like a maraschino cherry and get the fuck out of there. Once it was done, I vowed to never speak of the shit. But now you know the truth."

After a few seconds of silence, Amir finally reached out to dap up his brother. "All things considered, thank you for doing what you did, nigga. You were right for doing what you did, even if you were wrong about how you did it."

Ahsan pulled him into a quick hug and patted his back, a nonverbal acceptance of his brother's version of an apology. "You already know."

Zahra

S*ix weeks later.*

The bright morning light seeped through the open curtains, casting a sliver of sunlight across the comforter. I stirred as my lashes fluttered, the residue of sleep still refusing to let me go as I stretched my limbs. Seconds later, I heard a familiar, deep voice—my favorite.

"Happy birthday, baby." XL saddled up to me, snaking his arms around my waist.

I ambushed him with a delighted smile as I realized it was my twenty-fifth birthday. Six weeks had passed in a blur, and we'd fallen back into the groove of our responsibilities, but today was different.

"Thank you, baby."

"Of course," he replied, voice still thick with sleep. Heat pooled between my legs as he inched closer, shirtless and scratching his bearded jaw as his eyes pooled with desire. "You think you ready for your first present of the day?"

My eyes flashed with lust as I chewed on my bottom lip teasingly. "I sure am."

He rolled over on top of me, and I felt the hardness of his morning wood pressed against my thigh.

I chewed on my lower lip teasingly. "You're a naughty one, Mr. Patton," I quipped. "And I love me a naughty nigga."

"You already know," he responded before pinning my hands above my head with one hand while his other deftly slid across my skin, teasing me.

"Mmmm..." I purred.

He trailed hot kisses down my neck, making me shiver with anticipation. I let out a throaty moan as he nibbled on my earlobe. He was driving me crazy, tracing the outline of my bra before sliding underneath it to pinch my nipples. A low groan escaped from his throat as he abandoned it and found my center warm and wet with arousal. He slid a finger inside me. I arched my back against the warm sheets, crying out in pleasure at his welcomed intrusion.

He began to pump his thick finger in and out of me, faster and harder with each thrust. My walls clenched around him, desperate for more. His free hand found my clit and rolled it gently between his fingers, sending electric shocks through my core. I gasped for air, biting my lip, barely able to stifle my moans. The combination of his touches was almost too much for me to bear. I felt myself getting closer and closer to the edge.

"Fuck, baby. Yes! I'm about to cum!" I squealed.

Suddenly, XL pulled his finger out of me and let go of my arms, his hard-on pressing against my lower stomach. He pulled down his boxers before wrapping my soft, bare legs around his waist. I gasped as he entered me in one swift movement, filling me completely. The pain of the sudden invasion was replaced by an intense pleasure that shot through every inch of my core.

I moaned. "Oooh fuck!"

My eyes rolled back in my head as I rolled my hips against him.

"Shit," he hissed. "You feel so fuckin' good, baby."

My heart raced as XL's finger circled my nipple while his other hand gripped my hip, pulling me toward his body. I clung to his broad shoulders, biting my lip harder as more moans seeped through. Every thrust of his hips drove me closer to my climax.

The smell of our sweat and lust filled the confined space of the bedroom, mixing with the faint scent of the freshly washed bed sheets we'd put on the night before. The sound of our skin slapping against each other echoed off the walls, adding to the intensity of the moment.

"Oh fuck," I whispered, my head tossing back and forth as he pumped into me faster. "So good…"

XL groaned, grazing his teeth over the tender skin of my jawline as his hips met mine in a rough rhythm. His free hand trailed up my stomach, teasing my nipples through the thin fabric of my sports bra. I gasped at the sensation, arching into his touch as he pinched them, my back bowing.

The pressure built up inside me, each thrust becoming harder and more urgent. I couldn't hold back any longer.

"Fuck, baby! I'm gonna cum," I warned him, my voice strained with pleasure.

He thrust his hips deeper as he reached to pinch my other nipple, rolling it between his fingers. It was too much pleasure. My thighs clenched around his waist, desperate for more.

"That's it, baby. Cum for me," he demanded, his voice ragged as he thrust into me harder still. "You look so fuckin' beautiful when you cum."

And I did. My climax hit me like a freight train, shattering every thought in my head but the ecstasy ravaging my body. He pulled out of me and turned me around, hardly giving me a moment's reprieve before shoving his hard dick back inside me from behind, gripping my hair and forcing my head back.

"Ohhhh shit! Yes! Fuck this pussy, baby!" I cried out.

I squealed and moaned as XL slammed into me, his thick dick stretching me to my limits. His raspy breath was loud as he groaned, smacking my ass and increasing his pace. He gripped my hips firmly and began to pump into me, his thrusts hard and deep. Every inch of him filled me up, making me dizzy with bliss.

His strong hands gripped my waist, pulling me back against him with each powerful thrust. He hummed low in his throat, taking me roughly, claiming me as his own as he did every time he fucked me. His hips snapped forward, finding my sweet spot over and over again.

My eyes rolled back in my head, and a soft, high-pitched moan escaped my lips, muffled against my forearm as I creamed, unable to control the impulse to scream.

"Yessss!"

He slowed before smacking my ass again. Once, twice. It added to the sensation, the sting mixing with the pleasure as he took me again, harder, faster. I felt myself getting closer to the edge again.

"Oh shit. I'm... I'm gonna," I panted, my palms holding me up as my nails clawed the sheets.

"That's it, baby," he coached, his voice guttural. "Watch me make that pussy cum back to back like seasons."

The tension built up inside me with each powerful stroke, the sensations taking over my entire being. XL's rougher, dominant side was out in full force, and the adrenaline coursing through my veins only heightened my arousal. His hand landed on my ass again, this time harder, and a shock of pain mixed with pleasure shot through me, sending me spiraling over the edge.

"Oh fuck, baby!" I cried out, my orgasm washing over me in waves as my muscles clenched around his thick, long dick.

He didn't stop, though. He kept thrusting, driving deep into me as my body spasmed around him. Then, with a feral roar, he picked up speed, slamming into me with full force, his erection pulsing deep inside me as he came. XL's grip on my hips tightened as if he were losing control, and then he pulled me up, holding me against him.

We slowly regained our breathing before he kissed my temple, only laying me down but not releasing me when he was sure my legs were steady. The bedroom was silent once more. XL's strong, tatted arms wrapped around me, holding me tight as if he were too afraid to let go. I'd never felt so close to anyone in my entire life.

Finally, he pulled out of me, his softening rod slipping free, and I couldn't help but whimper at the loss of him.

"Damn. That... was," he panted, unable to complete his sentence.

"Yeah..." I giggled. "It should be my birthday every day, huh?"

He chuckled. "That's exactly what I was thinking. Now, go take a shower, and I'm going to work on breakfast in bed for you."

My eyebrows heightened with pleasant surprise. "For me? Yum! Okay. Off I go."

By the time I stepped out of the shower, I could already sense the day's promise as breakfast's warm, comforting aroma wafted into the room. My heart overflowed with love when I saw XL standing in the doorframe with a tray in hand. He approached me and offered up a grin, the tray loaded with a feast: fresh fruit, freshly squeezed orange juice, fluffy pancakes, eggs, bacon, and cheese grits—my favorite. I hurried to the bed, wearing only my towel and a cheeky smile.

"Happy birthday again, my love," he said softly before placing the tray on my lap. I looked down at the picturesque breakfast, admiring how beautifully it was all arranged. There were perks to being married to someone who loved to cook.

As I took my first bite, I couldn't help but reflect on how good it felt to be loved by XL. After the loss of my brother and my health scare, I hadn't been looking forward to celebrating another birthday, yet today was a beautiful reminder of the simple things that made life worth living.

XL went into the bathroom to shower while I ate, and my

thoughts drifted to him, including how happy I was. It hadn't been an easy decision to choose to stay married, but I knew it was right. I felt it in my heart. I looked back on our long talks at night, the raw emotions, and the vulnerability we both had to be willing to show for things to move forward. It was all worth it in the end.

Of course, I still had my moments of doubt. Our journey from marriage to love was far from flawless, but lucky for us, perfection had never been the goal. Survival was. And that was what we'd continued to do—survive. And in doing so, we'd built something frighteningly and wonderfully beautiful together.

As I finished some of my breakfast, I couldn't stop my thoughts from turning to my health. The recovery after my surgery had been slow, but according to my doctor, I'd made great progress. With each passing day, I felt a little more like myself.

The sound of my phone ringing interrupted my thoughts. I reached for it and saw it was half-past eight, and Doctor Ritter's name was on the screen. It was almost as if I'd conjured her up with my thoughts. I had half a mind to send her straight to voicemail. It was my birthday, after all, and I wasn't in the mood to hear any bad news. My heart skipped a beat, and my shoulders tensed as I pushed the tray aside and answered before she hung up.

"Hello?"

"Good morning, Zahra, and happy birthday!" Doctor Ritter's soothing voice graced my ears. "How are you this morning?"

"I'm doing okay. You?"

"No complaints here. I'm calling to deliver some good news."

Hearing those words, I finally relaxed my shoulders. "Yeah?"

"Your latest lab results have come back, and everything looks really good. You're still in the clear, and I couldn't be happier with your progress. With how things are going, you have a real chance at a long, healthy life," she proclaimed.

A rush of relief washed over me as tears of joy filled my eyes. "Oh my God, thank you so much, Dr. Ritter. Thank you for calling. Your news was the best birthday gift I could've ever asked for," I said, sniffling as I dabbed the corners of my eyes.

"Congratulations, and again, happy birthday. Take care."

"Thank you," I said before hanging up.

I hollered for XL as I raced to the bathroom, excited to share the good news. Luckily, he'd finished drying off and was standing at the sink shaping up his beard.

"Baby, guess what? Doctor Ritter just called."

"What did she say?"

"She said my latest lab results look good, and she's happy with all the progress I've been making since the surgery. She said I have a chance at a long, healthy life."

He brought a smile to bear as he set the clippers on the counter before turning to me. His face beamed with joy. "Wow. That's great news. I'm so happy for you, baby," he said, pulling me into a bear hug and rocking me from side to side.

"I'm so happy I don't know what to do with myself."

"You could always open your next gift," he suggested playfully.

My eyes ballooned with excitement. "There's more? Gimme, gimme!" I exclaimed, practically jumping up and down with anticipation like a child on Christmas morning.

He chuckled and left the room, returning moments later with something large wrapped in colorful paper.

"Open it," he insisted.

As I unwrapped it, my breath caught in my throat. It was a beautiful custom hand-painted globe, detailed with the words "You are my greatest adventure" written in gold script on the side. I traced my fingers over the rigid surface, mesmerized by its artistry.

"Wow, baby. This is beautiful. Thank you."

"The globe is just a symbol. I know how you're always talking about wanting to take a trip," he said softly, his eyes meeting mine, and he reached out to take my hand. "So, pick a place. The real gift is the trip. Anywhere you want to go, and we'll go. Anywhere."

My heart skipped a beat. "Anywhere? Are you serious?"

"Yup," he replied, his voice full of sincerity. "Anywhere you wanna go."

My mind jumped with endless possibilities as I slowly spun the globe. He was right. I did talk a lot about traveling and living life to the fullest. The world felt within my grasp for the first time, literally and figuratively. My fingers traced the shape of the countries and continents before pausing and hovering over Europe.

"Italy," I announced. "Let's go to Italy. Venice, Florence, Rome, I don't care. I know it's all beautiful."

XL nodded. "Italy it is, baby."

My heart fluttered. No one had ever done anything that sweet for me before, but then again, Kendrick Patton had been rolling out the red carpet for me since the night he decided to save my life. When it came time for Kendrick Patton to pick between life and death, he chose me. And it was the best decision he could've ever made.

Epilogue

Six months later.

I slowly opened my eyes as I rolled over in bed. Instinctively, I wrapped my arm around Zahra's waist, reeling her body closer to mine. My heart thumped with excitement as I realized our special day had finally arrived. Today marked one year since we'd said our generic vows in that random neon-lit chapel on the Strip. Our relationship had been a wild-ass adventure ever since, and now that we'd officially decided to stay married, I wanted to give her the dream wedding she deserved.

For months, I'd been secretly planning a surprise vow renewal. I went all out—hiring a florist to create a heart-shaped floral arch filled with nothing but crimson red roses and snow white baby's breath, arranging for her favorite love song to play when she walked down the aisle, and having a custom dress designed for her.

After kissing her neck, I quietly slipped out of bed, careful not to disturb her sleep. I trekked into the back of the closet where I'd hidden a beautifully wrapped jewelry box. Inside was a diamond necklace, a token of my love and loyalty.

I placed the box on top of my pillow next to a handwritten note that read:

"Do you know what today is? It's our anniversary. I have a whole day filled with surprises for you. Follow the clues, and you'll find me waiting at the end. I love you. –XL."

I couldn't wait to see her reaction when she found the note and saw all the things I'd meticulously curated to ensure her day was special from when she opened her eyes until she fell asleep. My lover's scavenger hunt would lead her to all the places I needed her to go, keeping her busy while I worked on all the finishing touches for our ceremony. By sunset, all roads would lead to a beautiful garden where I'd arranged a small, intimate ceremony with our closest friends and family.

With one last glance at the note, I recoiled my steps out of the bedroom. As I thought about the day ahead, I was hit by a wave of emotion. Zahra deserved the world, and I hoped she'd see how much I loved her and how grateful I was to have her in my life. I quietly strolled through our home, making sure everything was perfect for the day's surprises, and I couldn't help but think about how far we'd come in a year.

Our relationship had been a divine clash of paralyzing fear and unexplainable happiness since the night we met. Every obstacle we'd overcome had been beneficial to our growth. It blew my mind how effortlessly she made my house a home and how her laughter filled the spaces with the kind of joy that gave a real nigga butterflies.

Zahra's unwavering support had been my anchor as I took on the task of rebuilding my barbershop from the ground up. This time, on a piece of land offered to me by Ahsan to start anew. I poured my heart and soul into designing the new space, making sure it reflected both the history of my first place and the authenticity of its new, refreshed look.

The new building was almost ready, but I couldn't forget about my original shop. I couldn't abandon the old barbershop site since I owned the land and the structure that burned down on it. It held too many memories for me, my family, and the community it served.

Instead of reopening it in its original form, I decided to turn it into a place that could continue to give back—a community center for kids. I wanted them to have something we didn't when we were growing up and running around in the streets: a safe space where they could learn, grow, and, most importantly, thrive. I'd already started the transformation process. My cousins and people from the neighborhood had graciously volunteered to pitch in to clean up the debris before construction began. It was my way of ensuring the place that had once been my bread and butter would remain a staple in the community for the upcoming generation.

AFTER SHOWERING AND LEAVING THE HOUSE, I HEADED straight to my restaurant, where I'd personally curated the menu for our special day—baked chicken, fried fish, baked mac and cheese, green beans, collards, and garlic mashed potatoes. It was soul food with a fusion of comfort food, the perfect blend of flavors.

Satisfied that everything was running smoothly, I thanked my team and headed to my next destination—the tailor to pick up my custom-fitted tuxedo. As I tried it on, I admired the impeccable fit and craftsmanship of the designer fabric. I knew she'd love it, and I couldn't wait to see her reaction when she saw me standing at the altar waiting for her.

With my tux in hand, I traveled to the venue. The heart-shaped arch in the garden looked even more beautiful than I could've imagined. Ahsan and Amir were already there, helping to oversee the final preparations. They'd been a constant support throughout the planning, and I was grateful for all their help, especially with everything they had going on in their personal lives.

Ahsan had been working tirelessly on the next phase of his land development project, and the next grand opening was just around the corner. The latest phase would further address the homeless population's needs by bringing new affordable homes and things for the community, like parks and playgrounds, all a part of his vision and dedication to keeping himself out of the game.

Sienna was also celebrating a major milestone. After years of balancing her studies and her personal life, she was closer to graduating from college with her art degree. Plus, her artistic talent had finally paid off in a big way, as a few of her pieces now had a permanent spot in a prestigious art gallery in Paris. It was a dream come true for her, especially given that her blood was trying to sabotage her from the beginning.

Meanwhile, Amir and Nerissa were preparing for a different kind of venture. They'd recently shared the exciting news that they were expecting not one but two new additions to their family—twin girls. All of us were happy to welcome their little ones into the world, and Eli was eagerly awaiting the arrival of his new siblings, ready to tackle the role of a big brother.

As the three of us went over the last-minute details, excitement washed over me. Everything was falling into place, and in just a few hours, I'd be standing next to Zahra, the woman I loved, renewing our commitment to each other and celebrating the genuine love that had kept us glued together through the past year.

It was going to be a day to remember. I'd make sure of it.

ZAHRA

· · ·

Warmth seeped into my skin as the morning sun touched it. I stirred, my senses slowly coming to life as I stretched my limbs and starfished across the bed. The silence around me gradually gave way to noise, and soon, I heard the chirping birds outside the window. I instinctively reached out to XL's side of the bed, only to find it empty. That wasn't unusual. I was used to him waking up early to leave the house to oversee his restaurant and the two construction projects for his businesses. I rolled over, and a small, beautifully wrapped box on his pillow caught my eye.

Curiosity piqued, I sat up and picked up the box. A beautiful diamond necklace lay inside, the jewels sparkling under the natural sunlight filtering through the curtains. My heart sputtered in my chest as I spotted the handwritten note beside it. Smiling, I unfolded the paper and read it.

I squealed with excitement. "Oh my God!"

He knew how much I loved his surprises and little adventures. I raced to the shower and dressed before finding a second note on the kitchen counter next to a Greek yogurt parfait with fresh berries.

It read: *"Now that you're awake put some nourishment in your belly before heading off to get a pampering fit for a queen. I've scheduled you to get a manicure and pedicure at your favorite spa. Be there by ten o'clock. –XL"*

I closed the note and held it to my chest, feeling excited, knowing that he'd already made our day something truly memorable and that it had just gotten started. I couldn't help but wonder what else he had up his sleeve.

I felt pampered and refreshed after enjoying a relaxing pedicure, manicure, and facial. Just as I was about to leave the spa, the esthetician handed me another beautifully folded note that looked similar to the two back at the apartment.

I pulled a slow smile while eagerly opening and reading it: *"I hope you're feeling pampered like the queen you are. Now, it's time for the next part of your quest. Head to the place only fit for royalty—Caesars Palace. There, you'll find someone to help you get ready for the rest of the evening. –XL."*

My heart raced with elation as I left the spa and made my way to the hotel. Upon entry, I was greeted by a beautiful hair and makeup artist in the expansive lobby, eagerly awaiting my arrival, ready to beat my face and make me look stunning.

She led me to a hotel suite, and I sat down to let her work her magic. With my bombshell curls and soft glam makeup application perfectly executed hours later, I felt like I was glowing brighter than the sun. I was handed another note after I thanked her for her beautiful work. My heart pounded with excitement as if it were the first time all over again. I quickly unfolded it, eyes scanning left to right as I read it: *"Are you ready to have your wildest dreams come true? You're almost there, baby. Follow the man in the black tux upstairs for your final surprise. –XL."*

Engrossed in my journey, I followed an elegantly dressed man I'd never seen before, who led me to another private suite on a different floor. Without speaking, he opened the door and gestured for me to enter.

When I stepped inside, my eyes instantly landed on a gorgeous wedding gown hanging on display. I inched closer, noticing that it was perfectly my size. That's when it clicked. My heart flooded with emotion, knowing XL was giving me the dream wedding I'd always wished for but never dreamed of saying out loud. Tears of joy instantly welled up in the corners of my eyes as I reached out to touch the gown in disbelief. The final note was pinned delicately to the bodice: *"One final thing. Will you marry me again? –XL"*

His question, as simple as it was, instantly overloaded me with emotion. I couldn't wait to walk down the aisle and marry him again, this time in the wedding of my dreams, and reaffirm my commitment to the man who'd made our first anniversary a day I'd never forget. He'd set the bar way too high for himself.

I fanned my face, trying hard not to ruin my makeup with fresh tears. I quickly undressed and carefully slipped into the stunning gown. Each elaborate detail of the dress made me feel like I genuinely was royalty because the dress was fit for a queen. Once dressed, I took a deep breath and exited the room. My escort stood beside the door, and I followed him to the elevator.

My breath hitched as soon as the metal doors opened. I stepped onto the rooftop, still struggling to steady my breath while taking in the sight before me. The space had been converted into a romantic sanctuary, with twinkling fairy lights casting a magical glow across the perimeter. The floral arch was adorned with plush, full-bloomed red roses, their scent gliding through the air. The guests, XL's closest family members, turned to watch as I made my entrance, their faces beaming with joy and excitement. But it was when I locked eyes with him that the world stood still.

His gaze was charged with love and admiration. He looked the part of a handsome man who was madly in love and ready to renew his vows to me, the woman who'd accidentally captured his oversized heart. He was so damn handsome in his custom black tux that high-lighted his strong frame. A satiny red bow tie and polished black shoes complemented the crisp white dress shirt beneath his black tuxedo jacket. A white pocket square was neatly tucked into his jacket pocket, and a single red rose, matching the floral arch, was pinned to his satin lapel.

The corners of his mouth turned up in a tender smile as I saun-tered toward him, each step closing the gap between us. The tears threatening to fall all afternoon shimmered in my eyes, and I knew this was the beginning of another fulfilling chapter in our adventure. When I finally reached him, he took me by the hands.

"You look so beautiful."

"You look good yourself."

"Happy anniversary, baby."

I beamed. "Happy anniversary."

The preacher began the ceremony, and soon enough, we were exchanging our vows, this time with more conviction.

XL began. "Zahra, standing here today, I'm filled with nothing but the highest respect for you. A year ago today, we took a leap of faith and vowed to be there for each other in sickness and health, for richer or poorer, and in good times and in bad. Our adventure has been filled with many challenges and growth, but through it all, my love for you has only grown stronger. You carved an opening into my heart and put in a key I didn't know existed. From this day forward, I promise to continue to be your anchor and help you weather any storm that comes our way. I promise to protect and support you. I vow to love you with every beat of my heart."

He reached out to gently wipe my tears away. I drew in a deep breath while trying to steady my bucking heartbeat before speaking. "Kendrick, this past year has been the wildest, craziest, scariest, and most beautiful experience I've ever had. You've been my confidant, my sword, my shield, and my endless source of happiness. But you're more than my savior or my refuge. You're my teacher. Thank you for teaching me how to love again. Thank you for showing a broken girl like me that I'm worthy of a happily ever after too. Today, I reaffirm the vow I made to love you unconditionally and forever."

After exchanging our heartfelt vows, the preacher continued the ceremony and announced us as husband and wife.

XL pulled me into his arms. "I love you, Mrs. Patton."

My expression lifted in a smile. "I love you more."

Surrounded by the people who mattered most, we sealed our promises to each other with a long, passionate kiss, ready to write the next chapter of our beautiful love story together.

THE END

Afterword

A note from K.L. Hall.

Reader,

Thank you for reading *A Gangsta's Love Language: A Patton Brothers Spin-Off*. If you've made it this far, I hope you'll consider telling me what you thought about the book in the form of a **five-star review and/or rating**. Don't hesitate to let me know what you'd like to see from me next! I thoroughly enjoy reading your thoughts and hearing from you as well! I'm always striving to attract new readers and retain current ones, and reviews are one of the easiest ways to attract readers. If you loved the book, tell a friend, and most importantly, let me know!

All my love,
K.L. Hall

About the Author

K.L. Hall is a national bestselling and award-winning author. As a serial storyteller, Hall has penned over three dozen titles in various genres—including African American urban fiction and romance, paranormal, children's books (as Kimberley M.), and non-fiction. Her fictional stories straddle the intersection of classic Urban and spellbinding Romance.

Highly Acclaimed Titles:

In the Arms of a Savage: (Peaked at #1 in Women's Fiction)

The Potomac Falls Series (Peaked at #1 and #2 in African American Erotica)

Sign up for my mailing list to stay updated with new releases, giveaways, sneak peeks, and more! Click this link: https://bit.ly/38RMpV5

Connect with me on social media:

Facebook: https://www.facebook.com/authorklhall

Twitter: https://twitter.com/authorklhall

Instagram: https://www.instagram.com/officialklhall/

Website: https://www.authorklhall.com

Other novels by K.L. Hall:

Diary of a Hood Princess 1-3

Rise of a Street King: The Justice Silva Story (*Spin-Off to the Diary of a Hood Princess series*)

Broken Condoms and Promises 1-3

In the Arms of a Savage 1-3

Built for a Savage: Blaze and Camille's Love Story (*Spin-Off to the In the Arms of a Savage Series*)

A Ruthle$$ Love Story 1-3

Fallin' for the Alpha of the Streets 1-2

The Most Savage of Them All: The Wolfe Calloway Story (*Prequel to the In the Arms of a Savage Series*)

When a Gangsta Loves a Good Girl

Caught Between My Husband and a Hustler

The Illest Taboo 1-2

To the Only Thug I'll Ever Love

A Lover's Heist: Chief and Gianna's Love Story

A Lover's Heist II: Rome and Lira's Love Story

A Lover's Heist III: Baby and Skai's Love Story

Crushed Velvet & Cashmere

Crushed Velvet & Cashmere 2

Entanglements

Never Had a Bad Boy Love Me So Good

Good Girls Always Got a Thing for the Thugs

Professor Zaddy: A Potomac Falls Novel

Bound in the Arms of a Thug: Chop & Kendyl's Love Story

Make Mine a Gangsta: The Patton Brothers Book One

Gimme a Gangsta: The Patton Brothers Book Two

In the Arms of a Savage 1-3

Short Reads + Novellas:

Bi-Curious: An Erotic Tale

Bi-Curious 2: Tastes Like Candy

A Savage Calloway Christmas (*Christmas novella to the In the Arms of a Savage Series*)

Lovin' the Alpha of the Streets: A Valentine's Day Novella (*Valentine's Day novella to the Fallin' for the Alpha of the Streets Series*)

Awakened: A Paranormal Romance

As Long as You Stay Down

Solace in Seven

Solace II: The Final Cut

Something Bleu

Something Borrowed

Something New

The Knight Before Christmas: A Potomac Falls Short

I'll Be Home for Christmas: A Potomac Falls Short Book II

Triggered: A Potomac Falls Novella

Wasted Off You: A Friends to Lovers Novella

Because You Don't Know My Name: A Potomac Falls Novella

Will You Say My Name: A Potomac Falls Novella Book Two

Remember My Name: A Potomac Falls Novella Book Three

Every Thug Needs a Lady: A Lady and the Tramp Retelling

Ten Things I Hate About Lovin' You: An Enemies to Lovers Novella

In Exchange: An Urban Thriller

T.A.N.: An Erotic Novella

A Gangsta's Love Language: A Patton Brothers Spin-Off

Children's Books:

Princess for Hire

Princess Twinkle Toes & the Missing Magic Sneakers

Little One, Change the World

Adjust Your Crown: A Self-Love Coloring Book for Children of Color

Non-Fiction:

Authors are a Business: The Booked & Busy Course Mini Book

BLP

Howdie!

Thank you for indulging in a BLP book. As the ambassador of Black love stories, it gives me great pleasure to provide love stories regardless of the niche. Whether you are looking for urban romance, contemporary romance, erotica, women's fiction, paranormal, fantasy, or thriller... you can find an author to read and enjoy within BLP.

Now that you've completed this book, feel free to go to our website for a list of our authors to look up on Amazon and further enjoy.

With love,
    B. Love

www.blovepublications.net